Karaoke Nite
at the Love Club

Second Chance Romance

Book 1 in the

collection

Lucinda McFall

Shrike Publications

Albuquerque  Minneapolis

Table of Contents

Shrike Publications

Albuquerque NM

Minneapolis MN

https://lucindawritesromance.com

Publisher's Note: This is a work of fiction. Names, characters, places, and incidents are a product of the author's imagination. Locales and public names are sometimes used for atmospheric purposes. Any resemblance to actual people, living or dead, or to businesses, companies, events, institutions, or locales is completely coincidental.

Book Layout ©2017 BookDesignTemplates.com[1]

KARAOKE NITE AT THE Love Club/ Lucinda McFall.—1st ed.

ISBN 979-8-9876660-0-5

---

1.   http://www.bookdesigntemplates.com/

Dedicated to
DOC,
good doggie,
and all those great childhood beach memories. Meanwhile, the adults
were having their own fun. . .

"The heart wants what the heart wants. . ."
—*Letters of Emily Dickinson*

"Beach more. Worry less."
—Anonymous

Noooo!!!

"GIRLFRIEND. WHAT YOU need's a boyfriend." Gina's best friend Bunny was giving her that look.

"You know it." There went Gina's other best friend, Fran, piling on.

Gina Prine sighed at them both. Here it was again. The old refrain. She needed to stop their latest man campaign before it got started. "I don't need a boyfriend."

"Yes, you do." Fran said it first, but Bunny just behind her, the two of them joining in a little chorus of concern.

"I had a boyfriend. Didn't work out. And anyway, he wasn't a boy. He was a man—"

"A shitbag of a man," Bunny stuck in.

"—and I'm not a girl. You guys. I'm in my 50s. You think if Mr. Right was gonna come along, he would have done it by now." Gina summoned up a grin for the two of them. They meant well. "Let's face it. I'm an old maid, and I'm probably going to stay that way." She made her tone light-hearted.

"Old maid," sputtered Fran. "What is this, the nineteenth century?"

"No, really, girls. Listening to the two of you, it's like I'm your new project. I'm not. I'm happy the way I am. I love my life."

Gina found their raised eyebrows a bit infuriating. "I do," she insisted. "So." She hurried them along. "You say you have an idea for a girls' night? I'm all for a girls' night."

They were sitting cozily together in their favorite booth at The Mermaid, a lunch place that wasn't on the beach at all, but its name and décor were beachy enough. The three of them felt satisfyingly beachy there.

Gina sat on one bench seat of the booth, and her friends sat facing her on the other side.

The waitress came with their salads and iced teas. "Here you go, ladies."

"Thanks, Paula," said Fran.

"How's it going, Paula," said Bunny.

"Hey, Paula, Carly is a firecracker," said Gina. Carly was Paula's daughter.

"Almost more than I can handle, sixteen, sheesh," said Paula. She and Gina exchanged a look of profound understanding, mother to teacher, teacher to mother.

As Paula distributed the iced teas, Gina gazed around her at The Mermaid, its tired netting and cork float décor, its worn-out linoleum flooring. Over the counter loomed its wooden ship's figurehead with blurred features and sassy tail. Nice and beachy.

Gina loved the place all over again. She hadn't been born in Currituck Cove, North Carolina. She was a transplant from Maryland, practically Yankee-land as far as the locals were concerned. But Gina felt at home in Currituck Cove by now.

The town had its strand of white-sand beach, its picturesque weathered cottages on stilts, and one or two hotels—the rundown but charming Beach Club, the newer Seaforest with its tacky luxe. Just off the beach stood several motels of the franchise kind, and one beat-up No-Tell Motel out on the highway leading away from the beach and toward the town proper.

It was an old town, a sleepy town, and in Gina's opinion, that was part of its wonderful charm.

The civic boosters of Currituck Cove were always scheming—and always failing—to turn the place into a tony resort, a real destination, capital D. No one who really loved the town had worried much.

Until now.

Just this year it seemed the boosters might actually succeed.

Not because of the town's jewel of a little beach.

Because of the brand-new golf course going up a bit inland, designed by a famous golf course guru, Gina could never remember who. The Currituck Cove Chamber of Commerce was ga-ga over the new enterprise.

It was sure to attract a major golf tournament! A shiny new resort was going up just beyond the tastefully positioned golf-course condos and golf villas and fancy homes the resort was building amid the crape myrtles and the yaupons. Construction wasn't even finished yet, and already people with big money were lining up to buy the places. Out-of-state people, throwing down deposits for the houses and the exclusive memberships in the club. Resort-goers would get temporary memberships for a nice, stiff fee.

The whole town smelled money.

Gina held out a faint hope the peaceful nature of the town wouldn't get completely gutted. But she knew. If this well-funded enterprise succeeded, a lot was about to change.

Not me, though.

A sleepy Saturday in a sleepy town. Enjoy it while you can, she told herself.

Gina looked from Fran to Bunny, from Bunny to Fran, and they just looked at each other, not saying anything.

Gina picked at her chicken salad with walnuts, specialty of The Mermaid. Fran and Bunny picked at theirs.

Gina took a sip of iced tea. "What do you think of this new crowd moving in," she said. "Don't you think the new golf course and the new resort are gonna change things for all of us?" Talk about something else, she thought. Get their minds off their Gina Improvement Plan, and onto the hot topic of the day. "I doubt things will change much in my own life," she said, voicing her thought. "I'm guessing the people buying these high-end condos and McMansions and ponying up to join the golf club aren't going to be sending many of their kids to Zebulon B. Vance High."

"No," Fran agreed. "They'll be retirees, or people with older kids, or if they do have school-aged kids, they'll be the kind of people who send their kids to fancy private schools. Your art classes will be safe from them."

"Maybe you'll see some changes, down at the bank, though," said Gina.

Fran nodded thoughtfully.

"Not McMansions," Bunny interjected. "Don't call them that. Executive homes."

Gina and Fran rolled their eyes at each other.

"Me, I'll see big changes," Bunny went on, her eyes lighting up. Her two friends grinned at her.

Bunny was the Adorable Me cosmetics franchise highest earner for all of Currituck County. She was the only one of the three friends who drove a fancy car. It was one of the many prizes she had won with her sales savvy and hustle, and it was an unapologetic shade of magenta. She was the only one of the friends who had ever spent a week in Hawaii, and that too was courtesy of the Adorable Me Cosmetics Company.

Bunny Dowdy was a natural-born sales force of one, and when she gazed out across the Sound to the place where they could all just glimpse the lavish new clubhouse rising through the trees, the other two knew she saw green.

Green, green dollars, an entire new clientele with a lot of money to spend.

"But Bunny," said Fran. "Don't you think all those rich ladies will be spending their cosmetics bucks on some posh line of lipstick and nail polish and face goo they got in New York or, I don't know, Paris? Ow," she said, glaring at Gina.

Gina had just kicked her under the table. Hard.

"I'm not worried," said Bunny, smiling at them serenely. "Adorable Me has an upscale line. Did you know that? You didn't, did you. Adorée. And an even more exclusive line, Mélisande. It's never been worth my while to stock Adorée, much less Mélisande. Not in this little burg. Now it will be."

Gina tried to ignore Fran's skeptical look. It didn't unsettle Bunny in the least. "I know what you're thinking," she said to Fran. "You're thinking about me in some lady's kitchen, opening up my case on the kitchen table, and all the neighbor ladies crowding around, and how that's not exactly the scene I'll encounter in one of these chi-chi golf condos. But you don't understand." She snapped her fingers under Fran's glazed stare. "Fran. Think personal shopper. Think concierge. Think curated collection."

Gina began to giggle.

"What?" said Fran.

"Look at her," she said, indicating Bunny. "She's gonna do fine. She'll do great. Bunny has what it takes. The whole average income of this county is going to go zipping up, and Bunny's will zip up with it."

"I can't wait," said Bunny. "I'm going to open a nice little show-room and decorate it to the nines. But tastefully. And I'm going to ditch my nickname."

"You're going to reclaim Bernice?" said Fran, the skeptical note coming back. Fran had known Bunny Dowdy since kindergarten.

Gina was impressed. Bernice.

"Well. . ." said Bunny. "I was thinking Bérénice."

"Close enough. I love it," Gina declared, golf-clapping, but giving Bunny an affectionate grin.

Fran wasn't letting it go. She tried it out. "Bérénice Dowdy."

"I was thinking just use the first name," said Bunny demurely, whipping out an elegant business card, gold lettering, fancy script, the works. *Bérénice*, it read grandly. *Curated treasures for your personal care. Exclusive collections from Adorée and Mélisande cosmetics. New York. Scottsdale. Paris. By appointment only.*

"See there?" said Bunny. "Scottsdale. Great golf town. That will get some attention from this new crowd."

"Does Scottsdale even have an Adorable Me rep?" said Fran.

New York, maybe, thought Gina, fighting her own skepticism. But Paris?

"Course it does," said Bunny. "We're everywhere."

Gina and Fran admired Bunny's glossy little piece of cardboard, passing it from hand to hand.

"Well," said Gina, flicking the card back to Bunny. "Give Bingo a hug for me, Bunny. Kisses for my favorite doggie. I need to get going. I've got a still life to set up for Monday's class."

Two heads whipped around. "Oh, no, you don't," said Fran.

"Not 'til we've had our say," said Bunny.

Gina groaned.

"Thought we'd forgotten, didn't you," Fran goaded.

"Now look," said Bunny. "You know that nice place, the Seaforest, right?"

"Yeah." Gina's suspicions were rising by the moment. Girls' night? Or something else?

"Well, that's where the Currituck Cove Swinging Singles meet. In its ballroom."

"So?" Gina inwardly cringed. Swinging Singles. If that name didn't say Lonely Oversexed Geezers, what did?

"So next week they're holding a karaoke night," said Bunny.

"And?" said Gina, fumbling for her purse.

"And you're going," said Fran. She and Bunny had slid out of their own slick plastic booth seat at the same time Gina did, and they were blocking her path to the exit.

"Noooooo!" said Gina.

"Yes," said Fran and Bunny.

Can the pity party

"YOU'VE MADE ME LOOK at Hilton Head. I've looked at Bald Head. Figure Eight. Kiawah Island. I've even looked inland around Pinehurst and up in the mountains around Highlands and Sapphire Valley. All great golf communities, or communities close to great golf. What makes you think this is the place?"

Douglas McNally gazed around through the tinted windows of the Escalade at Currituck Cove's down-at-heels business district. He gave his best bud Theophilus Greene a wry smile. He knew something was going on in Theo's head. Something always was. The brainy roommate at college, the brainy one in a crowd of jocks.

"Well, first, the Carolinas. I like the weather better here than Georgia or Florida or Alabama."

"I'll be the one living here, Theo. Not you."

"I'll be visiting, bud. A lot. All of us will. And I do love me my creature comforts."

After all these years, Doug and his friends from college had stayed a tight little crew. All the friends would be visiting. A house at the beach? You know they would.

"Yeah, but why here." Doug waved his hand lazily at the window. "Why this town?"

"Worth a look," said Theo.

Doug grunted. "Did the rest of them put you up to this so they'd have a beach house to visit?"

"Wait'll you see." Theo laughed at his friend's expression. "These people around here are building an amazing golf course and resort, just up the road." Theo handed Doug the brochure. He nodded as he saw Doug's eyes widen when he spotted the famous name attached to the new course.

"You know," said Doug. "I read about this place in *Golf Digest*, and then I forgot it was on this stretch of the coast. You'd think I'd remember. I'm losing it, Theo." Doug sat back, squeezing his eyes shut against the bad thoughts that suddenly came crowding in. Jaclin. His dad. All the stress that came with them both. "I need someplace peaceful," he said. "Get myself back together." He gazed out the window again. "Looks pretty peaceful, around here." So peaceful it's practically dead, he thought.

Theo burbled on, oblivious. "Best of all, you can get in on the ground floor. Club fees before they shoot sky-high. Because they will, once folks discover this place. A fantastic golf villa or condo. Great golf. Great weather. The beach, just down the road, lovely place, unspoiled, none of these high rises, oh no sir."

"You're telling me I can afford Hilton Head, though. One of those other places. Anywhere."

"Built up, all of them. Overhyped. Overpriced."

Doug laughed. Theo was not only his best and oldest friend. Theo was also his money man, and damned good at it. Theo hadn't let Doug squander the money he'd made on the Tour, and with Doug's golf glory days behind him, Theo wasn't letting him squander it now.

Especially considering Doug's obligations. To his ex. His dad.

He and Theo exchanged a glance. They each knew what the other was thinking. One of the reasons Currituck Cove would be so perfect for Doug? Doug had just had to stash his curmudgeon of a father in a nursing home, and it was only an hour and a half away up in Raleigh. Doug's feckless younger brother had dumped the entire responsibility on Doug, even though Doug was in the middle of a messy divorce.

Their father. Doug grimaced. No one liked the old coot, to put it mildly, least of all his own children. Their long-suffering mother had gone to her well-deserved rest only a few years ago.

Doug's brother Stan had bailed. Doug had stepped up.

Doug understood why Stan wanted no part of their father.

But that meant the whole thing was all on Doug.

"Look, buddy," said Theo later that day, after many more conversations about the pros and cons of this location over that one, that one over this. "A house at the beach. What could be better? Especially—since this is you, the jock, not me—a house right on a golf course. But let's set my own enthusiasm aside. You sure you want to go ahead with any of this? You're taking a risk. What does Howard say?"

Howard was Doug's divorce attorney.

"Howard agrees with you. He says it's risky, but if I'm determined to buy something while I'm still going through the divorce, I'll have some protection from that piranha Jaclin because I'm paying for it out of my mother's bequest, and in cash."

"Risky, huh. Jaclin, she's a risky lady."

"My mother's bequest isn't part of marital property. It's safe from Jaclin."

"Not sure you should count on—" Theo began.

"Look, Jaclin knows if she messes with me, she'll be in a world of hurt. Considering what I caught her doing. I've got the evidence, too. Little thing she forgot all about. Nannycam."

"Nannycam?" Theo was incredulous.

Doug shrugged. "It's Pompom, her dog. She has only herself to blame. Pompom has a nervous condition. So Jaclin set up Nanny-cams everywhere, to keep tabs on the mutt while she was at work. Pompom doesn't like me much." Doug winced. He was outraged when he saw Theo was trying to suppress a grin.

"Hey, it was Jaclin's fault, not mine. She's the one romping all over our house in the nude with her boss. That so-called broker. She's the one who forgot to turn off the Nannycam. So that's why I'm not worried about buying into a golf community before the divorce is final. Jaclin and I have an agreement. I don't bring the Nannycam footage into the divorce, or bring up the, uh, incident in front of her friends, and she doesn't mess with me. Besides, she wants me out of our house. And I don't want to be there."

"Sorry I laughed. What on god's green earth did you do to Pompom?"

"Nothing," muttered Doug. "Dog just never liked me. Very possessive of Jaclin."

"Not too keen on dogs, are you?"

"I like dogs ok. Just not Pompom. Feeling's mutual."

"Where was Pompom during the incident?"

Now it was Doug's turn to suppress a grin. "Jaclin locked him up in the garage. Traumatized the poor little fluffball. Maybe I should bring that up to the judge. Animal cruelty." He stopped grinning. "I got that dog out of the garage. Me. His hero. His savior. And then he bit me."

It was too much for Theo. Theo fell over laughing. After his whoops of laughter died away, he gasped out, "Okay, Doug. Serious now. I just worry about you, bud."

Doug had started to grin again. "You're worse than a wife, Theo," Doug joshed him, not seeing the shadow that passed over Theo's face when he said it.

Theo said only, "You already have one of those. And what a piece of work she is."

"In my rear-view mirror, at least."

"Expensive," said Theo.

"I suppose. I give her a year, maybe two, before she latches on to some Mr. Moneybags. Then I won't have to keep paying."

"She's getting older."

"Jaclin's ageless, Theo. She'll look twenty-two into her seventies. A trophy who belongs on another man's shelf." Doug suppressed a twinge of pain. "I'm guessing she'll suck it up and bat those big blue eyes at some much older man."

"What about whatshisname?"

"The broker? Trey Nichols. A flash in the pan, that one," said Doug. "He doesn't have a dime. Just talked a good game. And he's young and buff, and. . ." Doug shook his head. "You know what? I don't know about this broker business. Trey Nichols says he's a broker. You ask me? He's a con artist. Anyhow, once Jaclin realized about ol' Trey, once she understood he's in debt to his eyeballs. . ." But, Doug thought, Jaclin had given herself one romp too many with the guy. Doug had walked in on them. And then it was all over with Jaclin.

"She tried making nice again."

"She tried. Not very hard. A no-go. It was over. It has been over for years. I just wasn't letting myself see it." Doug took a breath. "But you know, Theo, Jaclin knows it. She wants to move on as much as I do." Doug looked down moodily at his hands. "Especially now my career's over, too, and she won't be basking in all that re-flected glory."

"You don't know it's over," Theo said softly.

"Yes, I do. This is the year I'll probably drop off the Tour."

"You lasted a good long time."

"Yeah. Had a good run. Okay, where's this place you want to show me? Golf villa, huh. Maybe this is the place I should be put out to pasture."

"Don't talk about it that way."

Doug summoned up a smile. No way he should be inflicting his own little pity party on his best friend. Old athletes when their ca-reers are done. Could anything be more pathetic?

"I'll have to find a hobby," he said vaguely.

"Collect stamps," Theo urged.

Doug punched him in the arm.

"Here we are," said Theo, and their discreet real estate agent, pretending she wasn't listening avidly to every word, pulled into the brand-new complex.

Doug pushed the car door open, unfolded himself from the back seat of the Escalade, and stood up tall, shoving his hair impa-tiently out of his face. "What?" he said to Theo.

"Nothing," said Theo.

Doug laughed at himself. "I've gone completely gray, haven't I?"

"Looks good on you, bro. Distinguished," said Theo, his voice gruff.

"At least I have all my hair." Doug stood in the golf complex parking lot, his eyes roving over the new construction, really solid, and past it the immaculate fairway and greens, a beautiful rolling swath of ground. "Pretty impressive," he said after a moment. What was that look he saw on Theo's face? It wasn't pity, thank god. Something else.

"C'mon," said Theo. "Let's poke around. Then we can visit a few of the properties I've vetted for you."

So then Doug forgot all about that look, and the more he poked around, the more he liked the place.

The next day, he found himself signing reams of paperwork.

And the day after that. . .

The sun streamed in through the big windows of the kind of okay hotel where they were staying. The Seacrest or Seaforest or something like that. Doug woke up with a groan. His phone was beeping an incoming text from Theo. *Breakfast.*

Once Doug had showered and had shambled down to the depressing dining room, he took one look at Theo and groaned again. Theo the morning person, beaming behind eggs and grits.

"Don't give me that look," said Theo. "Sit down." He summoned the pimply young waiter over.

Doug sat back as the waiter carefully poured coffee into his cup.

Coffee. At least there was that. Doug raised the cup to his lips. Made a face.

"Well, aren't we the spoiled brat," said Theo conversationally. "The o.j's pretty good." He shoved the pitcher over to Doug.

"Can I go home now?"

"Go? This is home, bud."

"Yeah, but I can get back to Charlotte, relax a little before I head out on the Trail. After all, I still own that house."

"Jaclin's still in it, though," said Theo, giving him a look. "My advice? Stay here."

Doug knew Theo was right. What was the point of running into Jaclin again? There was no point. Sure, he could force Jaclin to move out. But the very thought of the effort it would take, the scenes she would throw, the drama she'd conjure up, the lawyers he'd have to summon, just made him tired. Still and all. He glanced around the little dining room. "My golf villa isn't even finished."

"Stay here and learn about the community," said Theo. "The more you settle in, the less of a shock you'll have when you really do move in. And moving-in day's not too far into the future. You go down to Alabama, follow the Trail, head to some of the big Tour events, then before you know it, moving-in day is here, and this really will be home."

"This little burg. Podunksville," said Doug under his breath.

Theo heard, but he didn't react. His face stayed bland and cheerful. "You should get to know this place while you have some time. Meet some locals. Do some shopping. You're going to need to furnish the new place. I spotted a great little antiques store out on the highway. Treasures going for a song."

Doug winced. He hated shopping.

"Meanwhile, over in Charlotte, Jaclin's getting her shit together and moving out, I assume?"

"Slowly. But yes. That's the plan. And you, sir, will be galivanting back to Chicago."

"Hey, bud. I'll stay right here. We'll explore the place together. Look. I'll do the shopping. You know I'm good at it."

"Aw, Theo." Doug was ashamed of the selfish joy that rose in him then. "You must want to get out of this burg. Go for it, man. You're right, I should hang around and get to know this place a little. But you don't have to."

"I know I don't have to. I'll do it anyway."

"Just hang around here?"

"Who knows, maybe I can help," said Theo with a sigh. "There's your Dad, for one."

"Oh. Yeah." Doug reached for his weak-ass cup of coffee and downed it. "There's that."

Theo slipped down in his seat, shaking his head and burying his face in his coffee. Then he looked up. "Doug, there's something else, isn't there? Not as earth shattering as all that other stuff, but still important. Buyer's remorse?"

"Yeah. I suppose." Doug glanced around at the drab surroundings. "But you know. It will be fine."

"It will be fine," Theo said firmly. "This one I can help you with. The antiques place. I live to shop. You know that."

Makeover

GINA DIDN'T THINK MUCH about her friends' threat: to drag her off to some karaoke thing. They were always scheming to set her up on blind dates, or trying to get her to join some online dating site, and Gina always fended them off.

At least she had ever since the night they convinced her to go out with Bo Nesbit, the owner of a fishing boat operating out of Corolla. Bo was huge, hunky, and maybe eight years younger than she was, and at first, everything was grand. Gina had to suppress a little shiver, thinking about Bo. But Bo had shown his true colors, and even Bunny was ready to throw in the towel on that little project.

Midweek, the friends' new Gina Project took an ominous turn. Gina got a call from Bunny.

"It's all set," Bunny said. "Fran and I are picking you up after school on Friday."

"Huh?"

"We're driving you to Norfolk, remember?"

"Wait, what?"

"We talked about this." Bunny's tone was patient. "Come out into the teachers' parking lot at 3:30 pronto. We're picking you up. We're driving you to Norfolk."

"Huh? Why?"

Bunny's voice, speaking to someone else. "See, told you. She's forgotten all about it."

"Is Fran there with you?" said Gina. "She is, isn't she."

"Yes."

"Okay. Remind me. Why are we going to Norfolk."

"Balayage."

"Buh-what?"

"Never mind. You'll see. You're gonna love it."

"Love what?"

"Your hair. And Johanna says she can work you in. They keep evening hours, at least for special clients."

That was Gina's first inkling that her life was about to change. Or anyway, her appearance. And fast.

On Friday after school, her friends swept her up Highway 168 out of North Carolina, over the state line to Norfolk, Virginia.

"I like Lurleen, in Elizabeth City. I've gone to her for close on fifteen years," Gina objected.

"Lurleen's okay. I like Lurleen a lot," said Bunny. "She'll understand, though. You need an upscale salon, and I know just the place."

By then Gina was resigned. Her friends were going to force her to go to this karaoke thing, and before they did that to her, they were giving her a makeover.

"Our treat," said Fran.

"Besides, I get a nice discount. I've made a connection with the cosmetologist at the salon this year, getting ready for the Big Cosmetics Revolution, you know, and now everyone there knows me."

"They must do your hair, Bunny," said Gina. "It looks great. I think I've told you that."

"Thank you," said Bunny, giving her blonde lob a fetching toss, and smiling.

"Okay, you two. I'm doing this thing. But don't you think you're going overboard, just a teensy bit?" said Gina. "I can see it all now. We'll go into that big barn of a room at the Seaforest, we'll sit down at a little table, have a few beers, wave at a few people we know, and then we'll go home. Why couldn't I have just gone to Lurleen?"

"Because you've had the same haircut for fifteen years," said Fran from the back seat of the hotpinkmobile. "The same one, and frankly, Gina, it drags you down."

"You're not making me go short, are you?" Gina felt an attack of nerves coming on.

"Let's just see what Johanna has to say. She's got a great eye," said Bunny.

"Time for a change," said Fran.

"All this for karaoke night," Gina muttered.

"Just the occasion, that's all. We're not making too much of it. Just the occasion for a fun change." Fran reached a reassuring hand from the back seat.

"And you're all gray," Bunny remarked.

"Well, yes. My idea, go gray gracefully."

"Nope," said Bunny. "Balayage."

"I know you've explained it to me. I still don't get it. It's just getting highlights, right?"

"Sort of like that," said Fran.

"I like your highlights, Fran," said Gina.

After that, Gina relaxed and began to enjoy herself. Her nice friends wanted to treat her to a nice haircut. Suppose she didn't like it. It would grow out. They wanted her to do this fancy haircoloring thing to it. Suppose she didn't like it. It would grow out.

That was the good thing about hair. You could make a big mistake with it, but it would grow out, and the world would not collapse into a black hole.

Actually, as the evening unfolded, she had a blast. It was a great idea for girls' night, and Gina was its star. She got a haircut, and the stylist, Johanna, was fun and reassuring. The balayage turned out to involve a really interesting blending of the gray in her hair with some lovely bronzes and ("Oh, god," Gina thought, although she didn't say it out loud) just a hint of lilac.

And a fantastic haircut, sophisticated layers that framed and feathered around her face.

"Like it?" said Bunny, after they left to go get drinks and dinner. White wine for Gina, a Manhattan for Fran, and Bunny the designated driver had club soda.

"Yeah," said Fran. "How do you feel. It's a real change."

"Love it," said Gina, and meant it. ("What on earth are my students going to make of this?" she wondered. But didn't say it out loud.) "Actually, I found the whole thing pretty fascinating."

"I knew you would," said Fran, nodding. "That's the artist in you, Gina."

"Haha, yeah," said Gina.

"And you look great," said Bunny, looking smug. "Well," she said. "I have to get back. Bingo needs his bedtime walk."

Bingo was Bunny's black lab.

At the end of the evening, when they dropped Gina off by the steps to her tiny front porch, the three friends hugged and laughed. "What a great present," said Gina. "What can I do to repay you two?"

"Earrings," said Bunny without missing a beat.

"Necklace," said Fran. "That interesting one with the green stones. I've had my eye on that. This whole girls' night idea was just my evil plan to get it off you."

"Done," said Gina. "Give Bingo a big kiss for me," she called after Bunny.

But her two friends were not done with her.

The next afternoon, they showed up on her front porch again.

Gina was expecting them. They were going to figure out what Gina should wear.

Gina opened the door for them. "You'd think it was Cinderella going to the ball, not some dorky local event at some dorky bad hotel," she told them. "Okay, follow me to my closet."

She and Fran sat on the bed while Bunny raked through the hangers.

"No," said Bunny. "No. No. No. Hmmm." She took out a dress, a nice blue that Gina often wore to church. "Uh. No." She put it back. Whirled around. "You don't have a thing to go dancing in."

"Dancing? I thought this was a, uh, you know. What's karaoke. Singing, right?"

"It's a party, girlfriend. Fran, you take her over to Modeste. I'm going to lay out my supplies."

"What supplies." That's when Gina realized Bunny had brought her big cosmetics case with her. The Adorable Me case.

"Don't worry," Bunny soothed. "I have a lot of samples. Some of them from the new lines." She positively sparkled at the thought.

"Suppose I don't want a new dress, Fran," Gina complained.

"You're buying one." Fran steered her through the front doors of Modeste, and Julie, the owner, was right there ooing and ahhing and already dragging out dresses.

"It's a conspiracy," said Gina.

"It's an intervention," said Fran. Julie and Fran had the bad grace to giggle.

When Fran hustled Gina back to her own house, dress bag in tow, and Gina saw the cosmetics ranged across her kitchen table, she got what Bunny called her "deer in the headlights" look.

Then Bunny went to work on her. Foundation. Contouring the cheeks. Blush. Eyebrows. Eyelashes. Lips. "And now," said Bunny grandly. "The coup de grace. The manicure."

"I think you mean the pièce de résistance," murmured Fran.

Bunny ignored that, and then she went to town on Gina with the buffers, the clippers, the nippers, the soak, the undercoat, the polish in a shade of daring scarlet, the top coat, and at last the little personal dryer.

"Pick you up at eight," said Fran over her shoulder as her friends rushed out the door.

"Don't chip those nails," said Bunny. "Or smear anything."

"I won't," Gina promised. She sagged into the kitchen chair. When she got up to go back to her bedroom and get dressed, and caught a glimpse of herself in the hall mirror, she almost screeched.

"This isn't me," she told herself.

But another part of herself whispered, "This is going to be fun." Then another whisper. "Maybe."

Woohoo

THEO GRABBED DOUG BY the elbow. "Look!" The two of them had dragged in from a long day down the coast checking out a great little seafood restaurant. They hadn't planned to go there; they'd wandered in for a beer or two and then stayed for happy hour and an early dinner, gorging on blue crab and Outer Banks shrimp.

"What?" said Doug. He'd had one too many beers. Hurrah for Uber. Or was it a Lyft? Expensive but under the circumstances, definitely worth it. "I'm all done in. I'm heading up to my room, watch a little tv, early bed."

"No, but look, man."

Doug looked. "Oh. Karaoke."

A huge sign at the front desk proclaimed KARAOKE NITE! TONITE! And then, in even more garish letters, FALL IN LOVE. WE DARE YOU. IT'S THE BEACH!

"Right here in the hotel. We don't have to go anywhere. It's right here."

"Uh. Karaoke. That involves singing."

"Yes, Doug. Yes, it does."

"Singing in front of people."

"Yep."

"Uh uh." Doug was shaking his head emphatically.

"C'mon, Doug. Be brave. It's fun. And it's right here."

"Uhhh."

"Hey, Doug. Remember how you said meet the locals. This? This is local. These are locals. You'll meet some."

"You go," said Doug.

"That's no fun, man. Hey. It's something to do."

In the end, Doug broke down and agreed. "Only if you promise me something."

"What's that?"

"You won't make me sing. No one will make me sing."

"Doesn't work like that. They take volunteers, they don't make anyone do anything, don't be silly."

"Okay. If you promise. But let me clean up first."

"Promise. It starts in a half hour. Meet you down here in a few."

Theo bounced off.

Geez, he's like a little kid about these things, Doug thought fondly. Then again, Theo had a great voice, and he was a real showoff.

"Okay," he told himself, psyching himself up for it. "Meet the locals. Make a fool of yourself. Yeah."

He showered and put on, what else, something from his collection of golf shirts, a nice relaxed jacket, a pair of khakis. Then meandered down to the hotel's big meeting place they'd labeled a "ballroom." The Dolphin Room. The kind of room with big plastic dividers that could turn the place into breakout rooms for a conference of orthodontists, or a smaller dining venue if you were a "financial planner" holding a free dinner to hustle up graying clients but not enough of them had taken the bait.

Right now, the dividers were folded back. The place was practically empty. The mc and some other guys were fiddling around with the sound equipment on a little platform at the front. Doug knew the guy directing the sound people was the mc because he was wearing a blazer with glitter lapels.

In front of the platform there waited a small dance floor. Strewn around the room, dainty round tables and a couple of big ones.

From the center of each table sprouted a number.

Doug's first impulse was to turn on his heel and get out of there.

A woman in a flowered dress materialized from somewhere, thin air it seemed, and rushed Doug. "Are you one of the new members?"

"Uh," said Doug. "Oh. This is a membership thing. Sorry, guess I got the wrong idea." He started backing away.

But there was Theo beside him. "No, ma'am, we're not members," he said past Doug. "We're staying at the hotel, and your event looked really interesting."

"Lovely!" she gushed. "I'm Suzanne. President of the Currituck Cove Swinging Singles. We started out with swing dancing, but now we've branched out into other activities. Our motto: have a good time. Welcome!"

"Don't we have to be members?" Doug mumbled.

"Oh, no," Suzanne the President said brightly. "We love new people. If you're just passing through, great, meet some of the wonderful folks in this town. If you're here to stay, and you're single, welcome to Currituck Cove and we hope you'll join our group."

She thrust a form at Doug, who stared at it open-mouthed. Theo reached past him and took it. "Doug is new to town, and I'm his friend. Theophilus Greene," he said, holding out his hand.

Suzanne shook it abstractedly but riveted her gaze on Doug. "New to town! Lovely!"

Theo nudged Doug.

"Uh, name's Douglas McNally."

"Lovely," said Suzanne with no recognition.

Thank god, thought Doug, relaxing a little. Not a follower of golf. This should be okay.

"Are you thinking of buying one of the new condos?"

"Just bought one," said Doug. "One of the little villas, actually."

"Lovely," said Suzanne. "Welcome to Currituck Cove. I'm head of the Welcome Wagon, too. Guess I'll be visiting you as soon as you move in. Those condos are nearly move-in ready, I hear."

"Nearly, yes," said Doug.

"Lovely," said Suzanne.

"Guess we'll find ourselves a table?" said Theo.

"Pick any table," said Suzanne.

"They have numbers on them. Reserved?"

"Oh, no," said Suzanne. "That's so the mc can call on you to come up to the mic. He has a lot of fun games he says he's gonna run." She beamed at both of them.

Theo took Doug by the elbow and steered him away.

"Theo. . ." Doug began.

"Shush. It's gonna be fun, just like the lady says."

They seated themselves at one of the little round tables, not too close to the front.

Out of the corner of his eye, Doug saw a bartender setting up a long table to one side.

"I'll get us drinks," said Theo.

"Club soda for me," said Doug. "That was one beer too many, this afternoon."

"But it went down so good," said Theo with a grin.

"Sure did," said Doug. He tried to relax. By now, a few others were filtering into the room. A couple, a group. The tables were beginning to fill up.

"Everyone's old," said Doug.

"We're old," said Theo, laughing. "But if you want to walk over to the local ice cream parlor and check out all the young beach babes. . ."

"My days around the young babes are over," said Doug. He knew Theo knew what he meant. Jaclin. All shiny-bright and twenty years younger than he was. Thirty when they met, but looking early twenties. And now Jaclin's forty, Doug thought blankly. Doesn't look it. "She'll do just fine," he said.

Theo's face turned from determinedly cheerful to concerned. "Still have Jaclin on your mind, huh. Too soon to put yourself out there?" he said.

"Nah. I need to take my mind off that. Off her. Besides, going to some lame karaoke thing at some lame bad hotel isn't exactly putting myself out there."

"You're right, bud," said Theo. "Jaclin will do just fine. And so will you." He ignored the part about how lame it all was.

"Here come the locals," said Doug.

The place was filling up fast.

"Hey, it's something to do," said Theo, looking around.

"Not exactly my scene," said Doug. "Yours either."

"Relax," said Theo. "It'll be a hoot. Now there's a trio of pretty ladies." He nudged Doug.

Doug glanced over. The three were settling themselves at a table. "Pretty," Doug agreed.

Then held his ears as a whine of feedback blasted the room.

"Welcome to Karaoke Nite here at the Dolphin Room!" whinnied the mc. "Welcome to the Currituck Cove . . Swinging. . .Singles!"

Shouts of "woohooo!" from the crowd.

Don't turn around

"RELAX," BUNNY HISSED. "This will be fun."

By the time the three friends had gotten themselves to the Seaforest, and into the Dolphin Room, and had taken their seats at one of the many little tables, the place had filled up. Gina recognized a few people from church, a few parents of her students, even a colleague.

"Ugh. Marvin Pugh," she whispered.

"Don't make eye contact or he'll be over here," Fran murmured. He had hit on Fran a couple of times. Marvin Pugh, the English teacher who thought he was writing the Great American Novel and let everyone know about it.

"Oh, hi, Marvin!" said Bunny brightly.

Gina and Fran flashed polite smiles and looked elsewhere.

"Ladies!" said Marvin. "Karaoke Nite, huh? Can't wait to hear those pipes, Fran." After a few moments, finding no encouragement, Marvin wandered back to his own table.

"But it's true," said Gina. "This event is made for you, Fran." Fran was a standout soprano in the choir of St. Hilda's Episcopal Church. Fran, sober banker by day, superstar by Sunday, had made quite the local name for herself, singing at weddings, the occasional funeral, anniversary parties, you name it.

"Made for you too, girlfriend," said Fran to Gina.

"Yeah, Gina, you have a great voice," said Bunny.

Gina, too, sang in the St. Hilda's choir. It was how she and Fran had met and become friends, back when Gina was new to town. Gina was an alto. "I mostly sing backup," she said. "Not like Fran."

"Altos don't get their due," groused Fran.

"Says the Star Soprano." Gina grinned. "This IS going to be fun. Fran is going to get up there and belt 'em out. The crowd's gonna go wild."

"YOU are gonna get up there and belt 'em out," said Bunny, giving Gina a meaning look.

"Oh, I'm not shy about singing. I hardly ever do solos, though."

"No biggie. This is just karaoke," said Fran. "Just a lark."

"You artsy people," said Bunny. "Singers, both of you, and then here's Gina the marvelous artiste of jewelry. I see you're wearing my favorite piece." Gina's bracelet was one she had designed herself. Gina was a jeweler, although her day job was teaching art at the local high school.

"I'd call you a marvelous artist, Bunny," said Gina, pointing to her immaculately made-up face, then her own.

Bunny made a *who, me?* little pout of the lips, but Gina could see she was pleased.

"Yeah," said Fran, bending over and scrutinizing Gina. "This has got to be your masterpiece, Bunny. Bérénice. Not caked on. Not too dramatic. Just right. Brings out Gina's eyes."

"Okay, guys, just when I was starting to feel comfortable, now I'm self-conscious again," said Gina.

"Gotta get over that, girlfriend," said Bunny. "Stop hiding that light under that bushel, as you religious folks say."

Gina laughed. "I'm not religious. I just sing in the choir."

"While I sleep in every Sunday," said Bunny.

"Hush, it's starting," said Fran, just as Bunny leaned over to whisper, "Who are those guys?"

"Who?" said Gina.

"Don't turn around. One really tall good-looking guy, man, don't turn around. And another guy, good looking too, but—well—my gaydar is going ping ping ping, so my guess is, he plays for the other team."

Gina risked a quick peek over her shoulder. Two strangers, one white, one black, both good-looking but one— "Yeah, the other guy, guess he's taken."

"Maybe they're a gay couple," said Fran, looking too.

"New to town," said Bunny, a speculative look descending on her. "Adorable Me has an entire men's line."

"Quit it, Bunny. No thinking about business," said Fran.

"I'm always thinking about business."

But Bunny's voice was drowned out by the mc. "Welcome to Karaoke Nite here at the Dolphin Room! Welcome to the Currituck Cove . . . Swinging . . . Singles!"

And Karaoke Nite got rolling.

The mc, while in Gina's opinion pretty cheesy, did know his business. He began with "Party in the U.S.A." That got the crowd into the stratosphere.

"Even all the old geezers," Bunny whispered.

"WE'RE the old geezers," Gina whispered back.

"Speak for yourself," said Bunny.

The mc played a few other energizing songs. Then the karaoke part of the night began, and first he got the whole room singing. Many, many crowd-pleasers from all eras. "We will rock you." "Sweet Caroline." "Don't Stop Believin'."

Gina was starting to enjoy herself.

"And now it's time! Let the games begin!" the mc proclaimed. That meant solos and duets and group efforts, and all sorts of little fun contests.

Just as Gina and Bunny—and probably half the room—knew she would, Fran wowed everyone. *Since You've Been Gone*. Naturally.

Even the despicable Marvin did himself proud, with quite a respectable rendition of *My Way*.

One of the two new guys, the one Bunny thought must be gay, confirmed it when he brought down the house with *It's Raining Men*.

"Great voice," Fran leaned over to say.

Everyone had joined in on the chorus, and now the room had exploded with applause, and it was clear the new guy was loving every minute.

Gina sang along with all the group numbers. And she let Bunny and Fran drag her onstage to do a smashing *Be My Baby* as a Ronettes wannabe.

A funny thing happened as she bowed to the crowd and stepped off the little stage. The man—that man—the other new man, the one with the distinguished gray in his hair. He was staring at her. Smiling a little.

Gina felt herself blushing. She looked away and waved to Mrs. Morrison, mother of one of her favorite and best art students, and got herself back to their table.

Bunny had brought gins and tonics to their table from the bar. "Drink up, ladies," she said. They had met at Bunny's house right on the beach and had walked over, so they had no worries.

But this drink is pretty strong, thought Gina. It tasted so good, also—late spring—it was pretty hot—that she downed it maybe a bit too fast.

Now here came Bunny with another round.

"I've got to go slow on these," she said to the others.

"Drink up," said Bunny.

Before she could think that through, Fran was tugging on her and waving frantically at the mc. "Here!" Fran was calling. "Right here's your volunteer!" And she was dragging Gina to her feet and shoving her toward the little stage. "Do it," she said, grinning. "Do it up right, girlfriend. It's the perfect alto number."

The mc assisted her up onto the platform.

"Now this is a duet," the mc was saying. "We've got ourselves the female. Who's our male? Who's our guy?"

That's when the fun gay guy was dragging his friend to the mic, and in spite of his friend's protests, too. "Right here!" he called out.

Shoved together with the very hot man with the gray in his hair, Gina glanced at him sidelong. "Guess we'll just have to suck it up," she said.

"Yeah, I'm not much of a—" the guy was beginning to say. Hot or not, he looked positively frightened. He was even sweating at little. "In fact, I don't even—," but too late, because the opening bars had them stepping up to the mic together.

The opening bars. *Total Eclipse of the Heart.*

"Don't worry," said Gina, underneath the swelling music. "This is not much of a duet, mostly a solo. You just do the 'turn around' parts, and look. . ." She fixed him with her eyes, trying to pour all her confidence into him. "Just SAY the lines. You don't even have to sing them."

He gave her a smile so grateful she wanted to kiss him.

They began.

At the end there was a big pause. He leaned into the mic, his voice husky. Called her "bright eyes," in the song's famous last line.

She thought she'd drown in his own eyes, gray, wide, intent.

And silence.

Guess that didn't go over as well as I thought it did, Gina was just beginning to think, when the cheering and applause began.

Gina and her partner were mobbed.

Bunny was sobbing. "I love that song," she quavered out. Her waterproof eyeliner was beginning to run. "That man. . .so sexy. . .the way he looked at you, Gina. Like he could eat you with a spoon." She giggled at Gina. "Old Southern expression. Doesn't mean what you think it means, girlfriend." She giggled again, a wicked giggle this time.

"Don't let her have another," Gina said, removing Bunny's drink from her hand and giving Fran a significant look.

The night ended.

The three friends floated back to Bunny's place. They all slept over. They all slept in.

"Guess it's a good thing that guest choir is singing in church this morning," Fran said as they stumbled around Bunny's bright kitchen.

"Just the same, we should have gotten ourselves there," said Gina, feeling guilty.

"Father Laughton will forgive us. They'll be around for that special mid-week concert, so we can redeem ourselves as good hostesses then."

"I don't want to talk about all that boring stuff," said Bunny. She had made herself what she called her special hangover cure, and now she took a big swig of it. O.j. with a raw egg beaten up in it, and

Worchestershire sauce. Gina had to turn away before she barfed. Thank goodness she hadn't had that second drink.

"Don't wanna talk about that stuff, no siree."

"What do you want to talk about, Bunny?" said Fran, rolling her eyes at Gina.

By that point, Gina was down on the floor, tussling the ears of her favorite doggie in the whole world, Bingo, Bunny's black lab. Gina didn't have a dog of her own. During the school year, she was up to her eyeballs in work for her classes and didn't think it would be fair to a dog to leave the poor thing alone all day and then ignore him when she came home. And during the summer, she traveled too much.

But she had Bingo for her surrogate-dog. Her puppy fix. Bingo was getting too big to be called a puppy. But Bingo didn't know that. And now he was trying to crawl into Gina's lap, all seventy-plus pounds of him.

"About that guy," Bunny was saying above Gina's head.

"What a voice, huh?" said Fran. "Wow. I understand he lives in Chicago, though, so I guess we won't be hearing him again."

"I don't mean that guy. I mean THAT GUY."

Gina stopped rubbing Bingo's tummy and stared up from her cross-legged position down on the floor.

Her friends locked eyes on Gina.

"Oh," said Fran. "THAT guy."

Dougie

WOW, DOUG THOUGHT AS he got himself back to his table after the duet with the amazing woman with the amazing alto voice. My knees are about to buckle.

"Stage fright," he said to Theo. Theo thrust a whiskey into his hands. Doug gulped it.

Theo shook his head. "Ice-water in those veins when you have to sink a putt so you don't walk away out of the money. But put you in front of a mic?"

"You promised, Theo."

Theo just laughed.

Doug drew a long shaky breath. What was happening to him? Not just stage fright. It was her. His partner. The way she'd looked at him, her eyes dark pools, mysterious somehow. And the scent of her, perfume maybe? Not just perfume. It was herself he'd breathed in. He felt again the touch of her hand on his arm, the feel of her as they'd leaned together at the mic.

I want to taste her, he told himself. I want to put my lips on those luscious lips of hers, and I want to— He looked up. "Theo. Someone's trying to get your attention."

A man was tapping Theo on the arm. A really good-looking man. Model good looks.

Doug couldn't hear what they were saying, because suddenly some guy in a plaid jacket was in front of him, right in front of him, in his face, actually, and Mr. Plaid was practically braying at him.

"Dougie McNally! I'm such a fan!" the man practically screamed.

Doug was scanning the room past the man's shoulder. Where were those three women? Where was the woman who sang with him. He needed to find her. There. The three were making their way to the door—

"Dougie McNally, who'd a thought it. Checking out our great new golf course?" the man in front of Doug yelled. "I knew I recognized you when you got up to sing."

As Doug tried to pivot around him, the man pivoted with him.

"Listen, Dougie. I got a few friends here—look here, Elwood, it's Dougie McNally!"

Surreptitiously, Doug wiped a few droplets of spittle off his face.

The swarming began.

"Hey, Dougie, hear you just bought one of the new golf condos up the road."

"Hey, Dougie, mind if you sign this?"

Damn, I hate anyone calling me Dougie, thought Doug. Resigned, he took someone's pen from his outstretched hand and signed their cocktail napkin. He signed it Douglas McNally. And someone else's. And someone else's.

Theo tugged at his sleeve in the middle of the scrum. "—party—" was all Doug could make out of what Theo was trying to tell him.

"Sure, go ahead. I'm going up to bed. I'm beat," said Doug, signing another cocktail napkin. "Thank you, I appreciate it," he said to the man holding out the pen. "Thank you." "Thank you, I'm glad you enjoyed the tournament." "Thank you." "Thank you, yeah, tough loss but I got by it." "Thank you."

He guessed he was used to this. Not recently, though. The whole time, he was slowly making his way to the doors out of the Dolphin Room, thanking and signing as he went. No point darting into the men's room. He knew from experience. Some of them would actually follow him.

So, resignedly, he got into the elevator and a bunch of them crammed in there with him. But when he made it down the hall of the sixth floor to his room, at least none of them tried to barge in too.

He did hear voices outside his room for a good ten or fifteen minutes, babbling excitedly. The golf club this. The golf club that. What a real golf celebrity could do for them. Finally the voices faded away.

He rang in to the front desk and listened carefully to the desk clerk's instructions about how to record an "I'm not available to take your call" message.

He'd started feeling like a hunted animal.

Not much excitement in a small town like this, he guessed. Not as if he were Arnold Palmer or Phil Mickelson. Guess people around here had to take what minor celebrities they could get.

Really minor, he told himself grimly.

He fell into bed.

In the morning, he blinked up at the ceiling, remembering. Remembering what he'd really wanted to do after the karaoke party was over.

Find that woman. His partner in the duet.

Thank her. She'd saved his butt. He couldn't sing a lick. But she'd showed him quickly and kindly what to do. Just speak his part.

And it had gone well.

I wanted to thank her, he told himself, firmly shutting the door to the other thoughts that were trying to push their way in. He wanted to more than thank her. He wanted to meet her. He wanted to gush over what a great voice she had, just the way those fans last night had gushed over him. And he wanted to—

He gulped. He thought all over again about her eyes. Her fresh prettiness. Her lips. The vibrancy of her voice, her presence.

God, she was a woman almost as old as he was. He always went for younger women, what was he thinking?

And look how well that works out for you, Douglas McNally, something cynical inside him said.

As he lay in bed, he had a strange vision of himself. A new Douglas McNally, shedding the skin of the old one. Rising up a different man.

He shooed the vision away. Shedding his skin like some snake. He thought of the woman again. He was aware his own mister snake had ideas of his own and was beginning to take notice.

I can't think about women right now, he told himself sternly. Down, boy.

I'm in the process of getting out of the toils of one woman. I can't slither into some other woman's garden.

The little cynical voice again: You just wish you could.

He glanced at his phone. Sheesh. He sat up fast. Almost ten.

By now Theo should have texted him.

He felt a burst of worry.

Then he lay back, smiling. Thinking about Theo's stunning performance, the bravery of it, opening himself up to an entire roomful of strangers, and how they loved it. The gorgeous fan who had tugged at Theo's arm, after. Theo, all excited about some party.

Theo was off having fun, or sleeping off having fun.

Doug was glad for him.

Just about then the text came.

Coffee.

"You're looking pretty rough, bro," said Doug as he slid his chair out from the breakfast table and sat down.

Theo groaned. "Late night. Very late night."

"Was it worth the pain? Tell me it was."

Theo glanced up from his coffee cup, which he seemed to be holding to his face and inhaling.

Doug saw no breakfast in front of him. Uh-oh.

"From the quick glimpse of him I got, that guy you went off with looked pretty hot," Doug tried again. He gave Theo an encouraging smile.

Theo groaned.

"That bad, huh."

"Remind me, Doug. Next time remind me I'm not a sweet young thing any longer."

"Well, your singing voice and showmanship are just as great as they always were."

"And my stamina and my head for liquor. . ." Theo set his coffee cup very carefully down on its saucer. ". . .are not."

The young pimply waiter came over

"Eggs," said Doug. "Grits."

"Stop!" begged Theo.

When the food came, Doug began wickedly wolfing it down. Revenge. Theo had promised not to make him sing, and then he HAD.

Theo turned green and left the table.

Doug had to chuckle. Who was usually the intemperate wild man of the two of them? Doug was. Who was Mr. Sensible? Usually? Theo was. "Tables turned, my man," said Doug under his breath.

Later on, when Theo felt better, they drove over to the new complex to see how Doug's construction was coming along.

"Forgiven yet?" said Theo.

"You promised."

"Yeah, but in the end, you loved it. Admit it."

Doug didn't intend to admit any such thing. Getting up in front of strangers to sing. Aargh. He could barely get up the courage to sing in the shower.

"Guess I should head back to Chicago," Theo said gloomily, as they poked around.

Doug thought again about his karaoke partner. "Aw, now," he said. "I do forgive you."

"Not that. It's just. I couldn't keep up with that hottie."

Doug wisely kept silent.

But Theo perked up when their real estate lady showed bearing floor plans. He started strategizing with her about conversation groupings and fabrics and wall coverings.

As they walked back to their rental car, Doug hesitated. Then he went for it. "Theo. Those ladies, remember the ones? The soprano with the astounding voice, and—"

"And the alto! Your duet partner!" Theo enthused.

"Yeah. Them. They were locals, don't you think?"

"I think so. Guess they could be tourists, but I haven't seen them around the hotel lobby or anything. Course they could be renting one of the cottages down the beach."

"Wonder if there's a way to find out who they are."

Theo looked up, suddenly interested.

"I just want to thank that girl. Er, woman. The alto. You know how I feel about singing, and she—"

"Yeah, she saved your butt, and in a really classy way," said Theo, looking appreciative. "With a voice like that, she could have made you look bad. My fault, bro. If I'd known what kind of voice she had, I never would have hustled you up there, cause, you know, she could have made you look bad. But she knew just how to get you in there and let you help her sell the song. Wow. You're right. She didn't just let you help her. The both of you sold the song. Did you ever. The chemistry, man." He shot Doug a shrewd look.

"I mean, send her flowers? But how can we find out?"

"Find out?" Theo looked confused.

"Who she is."

"Ohhh. Oh, yeah. That."

Doug looked away at the expression on Theo's face. "I just want to thank her."

"Sure. Of course. Okay, let me think. Locals or not locals? I know who'd know."

"Who?"

"Remember that lady, the greeter, the club president?" When Doug looked blank, Theo said, "You know, Ms. Welcome Wagon."

"Oh. Yeah. Her."

"She'd know." Theo whipped out his phone and tapped something in. "Here ya go." Theo handed the phone to Doug. The local Welcome Wagon web site, and a phone number.

Doug felt sheepish. He handed it back. "Nah," he said. "I'd feel silly, calling her. It doesn't matter."

"Well, if your partner in song is local, you're bound to run into her sooner or later, and you can thank her then. A town this small, you're bound to."

"Yeah," said Doug.

"Oh, c'mon," said Theo after a moment, urging the phone on him. "Put yourself out of your misery and do it. Call the Welcome Wagon."

"Nah, that woman will try to sign me up for her club. You know she will."

Theo sighed and put his phone away. "You know you want to, bro."

"Yeah, but I shouldn't."

"Jaclin. She'll be history soon. I think you should find her, Doug." And he didn't mean Jaclin, and he didn't mean Ms. Welcome Wagon. Theo knew exactly what was going through Doug's head. Exactly why Doug wanted to find out who his partner with the stunning alto voice was, and where she lived. Exactly why Doug couldn't do that, not right now.

They'd been friends for a long time, and knew each other well.

Shopping around

"C'MON. KEEP ME COMPANY," Bunny said to Gina the very next weekend.

"Oh, all right, but you know I'm no good at it."

Bunny was headed over to Maxine's, a great little antiques place and gift boutique out on the highway. Bunny was furnishing her new cosmetics showroom, and she wanted Gina with her for company.

"I know." Bunny sighed. "You still, even now, look like you moved into your house yesterday, and, you know, just dropped all your belongings and left them where they fell, and it's going on ten years. You still won't let me do over your living room. It could be so darling."

"I let you do me over, though," said Gina.

"And don't you look great." Bunny took Gina by the shoulders and swiveled her around. "Mark of a great haircut, it still looks good a week, two weeks, a month later. Johanna knows what she's doing."

"Yes," said Gina, feeling suddenly shy. She remembered how all her girl students had mobbed her last Monday, the first day of class after the big karaoke event. Gushing over how cute she looked. Everyone but JoJo, of course. JoJo just stood back with a cruel little smile plastered on her. Gina pushed that annoying memory away. It was the weekend. She was off the clock. She wasn't obligated to think of JoJo Gardner until Monday came again. Besides, the school year was nearly over. With any luck, JoJo wouldn't take art next year. One of those kids with no interest in art, but they thought the class would be an easy A and not much work.

Gina tagged along with Bunny to Maxine's. She half-listened as Bunny and Maxine put their heads together about Bunny's new showroom. "More than a showroom," Bunny told Maxine. "A luxurious little retreat."

Maxine nodded sagely.

Gina stared at them in awe. They knew exactly what they were doing, both of them. Gina herself didn't have a clue.

"But you're an artist!" Bunny protested when Gina pointed this out in an undertone. "How could you not know? What Maxine does, why, it's all about color and position and line. Isn't that what you do, too, with your art?"

Gina was a jeweler. It wasn't exactly the same as interior decorating. Interior design. She'd never know what Bunny and Maxine knew, even though Bunny's special passions ran to cosmetics and dress.

Bunny followed Maxine over to a furniture display.

Gina winced, thinking of the conversation she had overheard at The Mermaid only a few weeks ago. "That woman. Such a dumpy little thing, no style at all." The voice was floating over from the booth behind her, and Gina suddenly realized the voice was talking about HER. "Well, she's a Yankee, after all." In cutting tones.

Now why should she be torturing herself about that particular vicious little comment? she berated herself, drifting among all Maxine's lovely finds.

Oh, she thought. She suddenly knew why. Because the voice had turned out to belong to Amelia Gardner. JoJo's pushy mother, the ultimate helicopter parent. The ultimate Junior League snob. Gina had been thinking of JoJo, and now she was thinking of JoJo's hateful mother's hateful words. Get out of my head! she silently cried at them both.

Suddenly Bunny was standing in front of her. "Gina. You know you have a great sense of style, don't you?"

Gina looked up startled. Was Bunny a mind-reader? Then she realized Bunny was just, in quintessential Bunny fashion, continuing the conversation Gina had started earlier, about how useless Gina would be to Bunny during a visit to Maxine's.

"You have a fun bohemian sense of style, Gina Prine. It's not the sense of style all these Southern ladies around here flaunt, and not the sense of style I need for my new digs, not if I'm going to sell to this new clientele. But it's yours, Gina, and it's great."

Gina giggled at how earnest Bunny was sounding.

Then Maxine called her away to compare two swatches of fabric, and Gina browsed aimlessly on.

After a while, she started to get itchy. Sorry she'd agreed to come. She was getting bored. She reached over and hefted two gilded pineapple bookends. Bookends for people who didn't read many books.

Behind her, a man was talking. Talking to Bunny, she suddenly realized. Gina carefully replaced the bookends.

Talking about. . .

Gina whirled around.

Karaoke Nite!

"I loved, loved, loved that number you sang. You really rocked it," Bunny was saying.

"Hey, and you were the third Ronette!" the man was gushing back at Bunny.

Bunny giggled. "The Third Ronette! I love it! Yeah, just me, the least-talented of the three."

It was that man! The one who had sung *It's Raining Men!* The friend of—

And here Gina stopped and blushed hard. She shrank back among the decorative tea towels.

"I didn't mean that the way it came out," said the man, sounding abashed.

Bunny laughed. "No offense at all. My two friends are the singers. I'm just a good sport. I can't sing."

"Your two friends were amazing. Are you three from around here?"

"Yep," said Bunny. Gina watched, mesmerized, as Bunny handed a little card to the man. "That's me. Bérénice. But my friends call me—" another patented Bunny giggle—"Bunny."

"Pleased to meet you, Bunny. I'm Theophilus Greene."

"You and your friend are visitors, I take it," said Bunny, smooth as could be.

No, Bunny! Gina groaned inside. Why had she confessed to Bunny how much she liked this man's friend, and how much she wanted to know where they were from, and how long they were staying, and—

"I'm visiting from Chicago," said this man, Theophilus Greene. "But my friend is moving into one of the new golf course homes. Doug McNally. So he's about to become your neighbor."

And is he gay? thought Gina. But she didn't think he was. Doug, she said to herself. She thought about the sexy vibes practically radiating off him, as they performed their duet and he began to relax and enjoy himself. Not gay.

Bunny's shriek interrupted these thoughts. "Doug McNally! THE Doug McNally? As in, Douglas McNally the golfer?"

"That's the man," said Theophilus Greene, not a bit disconcerted.

"Why didn't I recognize him? Doug McNally. Right there at Karaoke Nite."

"Guess that's the last person you expected to see at Karaoke Nite," said Doug's friend.

"That's it. We see what we expect to see," said Bunny, nodding her head wisely.

"Listen, Bunny. Bérénice," said the friend. "Doug has really, really in the worst way wanted to find out who. . ." Here the friend's voice dwindled as he followed Bunny over to another rack of upholstery swatches.

Gina found herself leaning to hear what they were saying.

Over went the whole tea-towel display with a crash.

Maxine was there, tidying up, reassuring Gina. "No harm done, sweetie," she was saying.

And Bunny and the *Raining Men* guy had swiveled around, fixing her in their fascinated gaze.

"Oh," said Gina. She could feel herself blushing furiously.

"And there she is," said Bunny triumphantly. "Gina, get over here. This nice man is a big fan of yours. He wants to meet you." She inclined her head to the man. "Theophilus Greene," she said.

Maxine was nodding, making sure she got in on the conversation. "Karaoke Nite. I heard about that."

Theophilus Greene bounded over to Gina and took her by both hands. "Gina Prine! The superstar of the evening!"

Gina was able to laugh. Sort of. "No," she got out. "I think that honor belongs to you, Mr. Greene."

"Theo. Please. And thanks, but no, it was you all the way."

Gina's fascination was beginning to replace her horrible embarrassment. "You were so good at it. You sold that song. Are you—"

"Oh," said Theo dismissively. "When I was younger, I went for a career in musical theater. But you know, that's such a long shot. I guess my practical side got the better of me. I'm a CPA."

"I just sing in the church choir," said Gina. "So does Fran, our friend. The soprano," she prompted.

"And you're both damned good at it, too," said Theo. It was his turn to look embarrassed. "Pardon the language."

"Ha. I'm not very churchy. I just love to sing," said Gina.

Theo stood there gazing down at her. "So much talent," he said softly. "It's a shame, isn't it, all this talent hidden away."

"But your friends appreciate it," said Bunny, cutting in. "Singing's not even Gina's main talent. She's an artist. A jeweler."

"So much talent, wow." Theo grabbed up Gina's arm and stared at her wrist. "You make this? I was looking at this."

"Yes," said Gina.

"And these," said Bunny, flaunting her new earrings.

"Wow," said Theo. "Uh, Gina. . .Ms. Prine. . .you remember my friend Doug, the one you rescued at Karaoke Nite?"

"Sure she does," said Bunny before Gina could get her mouth open.

"He'd love to meet you and thank you. Wouldn't know it about the guy, but he is real shy where these things are concerned. And you really saved his butt. . .er. . self-esteem."

They all laughed. Gina looked aside at Maxine, who was laughing along and fidgeting a little, too.

But once both Bunny and Theo turned their minds to business, the business that had brought them both there, Maxine's fidgeting turned to beaming. Bunny was there to furnish her showroom. Theo was there to furnish his friend's condo. Bunny and Theo saw in each other a kindred spirit. And Maxine saw the satisfying flash of dollar signs.

"You know," Theo leaned over to Bunny to say, while Gina stared up at some paintings of fruit and flowers and wondered who could possibly find them very interesting, "I overheard you talking to Ms. Maxine about your ideas, and I thought, now THERE's a brain I'd like to pick."

Bunny made some sort of appreciative noise.

"And then," Theo went on, "I recognized you. And then—" They both turned to Gina, who tried to pretend she wasn't furiously eavesdropping. "—I recognized her, and I realized. . ." Here his voice dropped. Gina could only pick out the word "Doug."

At the end of a good long hour, while Gina was about to die of either boredom or curiosity, whichever came first, Bunny was at last at the counter with Maxine to place her orders and make her purchases. Theo was right behind her with his own orders and purchases.

As they all bundled out the door together, Theo turned to Gina.

"Gina," he said. "Do you happen to have thirty minutes or an hour? Bunny, can you spare Gina for a little while? I promise to bring her back."

That's how Gina found herself in Theo's rental car. "I picked Bunny's brain. Now I want to pick yours."

"What about?" said Gina.

"Well. I love Maxine's taste, and I know all the wall art in her place is perfectly tasteful." Theo was driving them toward. . .

Gina peered through the windshield. Looked like they were heading for the new golf and resort complex.

"Yes, it is tasteful, I suppose, but—"

"Exactly," said Theo, reading her mind. "Doug hates shopping and all that stuff, so he has put me in charge of furnishing his golf course home. And I think he should have some real art on his walls, not just art that matches his upholstery. He needs art from the region. North Carolina, maybe South Carolina and Virginia. Correct me if I'm wrong, Ms. Prine, but I'm guessing you'll know a ton of artists from this region."

"Yes," said Gina. "I do. I don't paint, except for my own pleasure. But I know a lot of painters. I know a woman who makes exquisite little drawings. I know some great print makers. All that. I can give you a list of them. Take you to see some of them, if you'll be around a while."

"I knew it!" Theo beamed at Gina. "I can tell from your jewelry. You have a great eye. Here we are." He swung the car into the parking lot of the new complex, got out, and ushered Gina out of the car.

"Also," he said, his voice dropping, "There's someone who wants to thank you, and there he is, standing right over there."

Good eye

THE MOMENT DOUG LOOKED down into those big beautiful brown eyes, he knew. He knew he was some kind of crazy man, because what he felt was not the normal thing, not for him. He knew the woman he wanted. Not some bimbo. Not some trophy. Gina Prine.

It was the second time he'd looked into those eyes, true, the second time he'd found himself drowning in them.

A little puzzled look was descending on her.

He licked his lips. Say something, fool! "I want to thank you," he got out. "For karaoke night."

"To tell the truth, my friends had to drag me there kicking and screaming," she said lightly.

What a voice, he thought. Her speaking voice, like her singing voice. It was honey. No Southern drawl. Just. . . honey.

"So you're not, uh, a member of the Currituck Cove Swinging Singles?"

"The Love Club?" She laughed. "That's what we locals call it. That group has always seemed kind of desperate to me. But, well, my friends wanted to sing karaoke, and I gave in and went with them."

"Sure am glad you did. What if you hadn't. My best friend betrayed me." He mock-glared at Theo, hovering with a grin just past them. "He promised me he wouldn't make me sing, because he knows what a chicken about stuff like that I am, and then he shoved me right up on that stage in front of all those strangers."

"And you did just fine," she said.

"Thanks to you."

"Well—" She cleared her throat.

She's about to leave, and I don't want her to, but I don't have anything else to say, he thought in panic. "You have a great voice," he blurted out.

"Thank you," she said.

If only he'd had a little cocktail napkin and a pen, he'd stick it under her nose and make her sign it for him. Her adorable little nose. For the first time, he sympathized with all those fans who chased him down, not that he had many of those any more.

Theo rescued him. As always. Smooth customer that he was. "I knew you wanted to thank Gina, but that's not the real reason I brought her over," he said.

Sure it isn't, thought Doug. But as it turned out, Theo really did have another reason.

"Gina is an artist."

"You sure are," he told her.

"I don't mean the singing, although she's great at that too. She does other kinds of art."

"Oh?" said Doug.

"She knows people, Doug, good buddy. People whose art you have to see. People whose art you're gonna want on your walls."

"But you're the artist. What about your own art, Gina? Will you let me see it?"

Gina raised her arm and rattled the bracelets on it, smiling at Theo.

"I don't get it," said Doug.

"Thick, isn't he?" said Theo to Gina. "Gina is a jeweler," he said to Doug. "That kind of artist. But she knows all the other kinds."

"So you and Gina are going to scour the state for something I can put on my walls," said Doug, finally clued in.

"I thought you should come along with us."

"I don't really know much about art."

"Gina will teach us both about the art in this region," said Theo, giving Doug a look that said, YOU REALLY ARE THICK, BRO.

"Oh," said Doug. "Sure. I'd love that. If you have the time, Gina."

"It will be my pleasure," said Gina.

Gina was as good as her word. She kept them both focused, especially once the school year was over only weeks later. Every few mornings, Theo and Doug swung by in the rental car to pick her up.

They'd visit small galleries. The homes of artists. Barns where someone had stashed art he didn't know what to do with. They went all over coastal North Carolina. Coastal Virginia.

In the morning, Theo and Doug would drive over to pick Gina up. She'd rush out after her cup of coffee and cereal, and hop in back. Then they'd head out.

Those mornings with Gina. They were magical. Doug learned more about art than he ever knew he needed to. By the end of the first week, he didn't just need to. He wanted to. Anything, to stay near her.

There was something about her.

She was cute, definitely cute. But not some glamorous babe. Doug struggled to figure out what it was about her that so enticed him.

She looked little. Fragile. She was anything but. She had a stamina and energy that floored him. And what a great eye.

She'd take him into some dusty small-town gallery, march him straight up to a neglected-looking painting on a far wall, and point. "There," she'd say. "That one's amazing." What an eye.

Doug figured he could buy some of these works for a song, and Gina assured him he could. "Just offer her something reasonable. She'll bite," Gina said of one artist.

When it came time to open his wallet, though, Doug did a really un-Doug-like thing. He insisted on paying full price. He realized he was beginning to worship these artists a little. They could do such astounding things, and mostly the world didn't reward them for it. Didn't even notice. Doug felt that was a crime.

Look at his own talent. Even coming in at the bottom of the board, as he had for the last years, his income had been adequate. Of course, as a young up-and-comer he'd once had to fight hard for his spot on the Tour. Many talented golfers gave up before they reached that point—golfers maybe more talented, in the raw sense, than he was. But he was the one who'd had the hunger. They had not.

That was something he recognized in these artists now. Theo agreed with him there.

"I had the talent for musical comedy," Theo said once, looking a little sad. "I was the genuine triple threat. Singing. Dancing. A flair for comedic acting. I sold out, though, once I realized what a long shot it was to keep chasing that dream. But these folks!" They had pulled up into the rutted yard of some country person's tumbledown house. Gina had told them a home studio was out back. Theo waved his hands around. "These folks. These artists. They keep going."

Doug smiled at Theo, remembering their college days, when Theo was the star of every single college theater production. "You were really good, Theo," said Doug. "Fiddler on the Roof. Guys and Dolls. How to Succeed in Business. If it had been on Broadway, Theo was in it, and usually in the lead role," he explained to Gina.

"Except that time we tried *Hamlet*," said Theo, grimacing. "Hamlet. That's. . .not me."

Gina laughed. "To be Theo, or not to be Theo. That is the question."

Theo laughed along. "As it turns out, what I am's a damn good CPA."

"Not only that, Theo," said Doug. "A damn good friend. You could be in Chicago, tending to your other clients."

"Oh," said Theo. He patted his laptop on the passenger seat. "I can be anywhere in the world and still tend to them. And I do."

Somehow, that day Doug had wound up in the back, with Gina. He looked aside to her hand, resting on the space between them. He thought about what would happen if he picked it up. Caressed it. Kissed it.

"Ready?" said Gina, halfway out her door, looking back at him puzzled.

"Oh," said Doug. "Wool-gathering. Sure."

In late May, though, Doug left for the championship. "Still on the Tour," he said, trying to be cheerful. Wondering if it would be his last year. At least he still had his tour card. Barely. Of course, once, a long time ago, he had indeed lost it. But that was just bad luck, happened to everyone, and Doug had clawed it back. Now, though. Now he was too damned old. A career in professional golf might last longer than most professional athletes'. But it couldn't go on forever.

He was standing on Gina's tiny front porch. He'd come by her house to tell her goodbye. "I'll miss our art field trips," he told her.

"Me too," she said. "That's my passion. But now you're heading off to your own passion. I don't know a thing about golf."

"I know."

"Good luck! Theo tells me he'll keep me informed about how you do."

"You can watch some of it on tv, you know."

"I'll have to get Theo to tell me when. Then he'll have to give me the play-by-play."

Doug had to grin at that.

"Blow-by-blow? Putt-by-putt?" she tried.

"Well," he said, swallowing hard. "I'll be back when the season's over, and by then my house will be ready. Looking forward to some winter golf around here."

"Have a good flight."

Fool, he told himself. Kiss her.

He grabbed her and did it. As his lips met hers, as he inhaled her scent, as he felt her own lips meet his and how soft they were, how they slightly parted, he wanted desperately to thrust his tongue into her mouth and taste her and explore her. And his dick wanted it, too. It had hardened against her thigh as he pulled her toward him. It had definite ideas of its own.

He stood still in shock at his own need.

She pulled away. Slowly. "Wow."

"I've been wanting to do that for a long time," he whispered at her ear.

"Um. Theo tells me you're married."

"Did Theo tell you I'm going through the last months of a divorce?"

She shook her head no. "I think he let it slip, the thing about being married. He's not very gossipy, Theo." She looked down. The thickest lashes. "I guess I wondered, though. You're buying this condo, or whatever you call it, and Mrs. Doug is never around."

"Mrs. Doug is history."

"Not quite," she said, giving him a hug. Briskly, this time. Maneuvering his insistent body away from hers. A hug that said FRIENDS. And nothing more. "Hope you do really well on the tour."

"We'll see." He turned away, hoping his erection wasn't as obvious as he knew it was. He limped to his car and got in, sweating. Wanting to leap back out of it and take her into his arms and make her sweetness all his.

Instead, he steered away from her house, forcing himself not to look back. He made toward the highway, and then to Norfolk, to catch his plane. But he ached for her the whole way.

Which hug was the real hug?

The first one, when she leaned against his body so softly he felt himself shudder with the forbidden urge to possess her.

Or the second one, relegating him firmly to friend zone.

He got on the plane still wondering. Still aching.

Blaze of glory

GINA KNEW SHE WAS BEHAVING foolishly, but she couldn't get over that kiss. The feel of Douglas McNally pressing against her. Just thinking about that got her bothered all over again. She felt a guilty jolt as she remembered the night before, when she'd found herself fantasizing about him.

She ended up touching herself. Touching her breasts, her sex. Trying to recapture the feeling it gave her, when he stood so close, his desire so obvious. Her own desire, as it flared up in answer. I'm acting like a horny teenager, she marveled. How long had it been since a man made her feel like that?

Now, ensconced in a Mermaid booth, she looked over at her friends, wondering if they could tell how guilty she felt. Just looking at her, wondering if they could tell how much she desired what she couldn't have. "He's a married man," she scolded herself. Then she said it out loud.

"Sounds like he won't be for long," said Bunny. The Her two friends could tell something was bothering her, and now Gina had spilled it.

"You never know, do you? Some people start a divorce, and then they think better of it. Besides." Gina took a gulp of her iced tea. "Even when his divorce goes through—if it does—he'll be a man on the rebound, and everyone knows how dangerous those are."

"Not very trusting, is she?" said Fran to Bunny.

Gina wasn't sure about trusting Douglas McNally, but she sure as hell didn't trust herself. She realized she'd never told her friends one reason for her deep mistrust. When she'd first moved to Currituck Cove, she'd told everyone in town she moved there to give herself a change. Just wanted to live at the beach. Everyone bought that. Who doesn't want to live at the beach?

But Gina's main reason for moving from Maryland to Currituck Cove was to get away from a relationship that had gone very wrong. A relationship with a man who was married. And had lied about it. When she allowed herself to think about Holt at all, the illicit feelings floored her. Betrayed her. So she kept them tightly locked into some compartment with the word FORBIDDEN stamped on it in big red letters.

Only later did she and Fran and Bunny become friends, and her real reason for moving to their town had never come up. By then, or so she had told herself, that toxic situation was ancient history.

Also, she was ashamed of herself. I should have seen the signs, she told herself bitterly, trying to keep that old hurt away.

"Gina," said Fran, putting down her iced tea. Looking over at Gina with concern. "Somebody hurt you, Gina. Hurt you bad."

"Yeah," Gina said, and tried to laugh. "How is it you two are both mind-readers. That was a long time ago."

"A married man?" Bunny guessed.

Gina nodded dumbly.

"Loser. Doing a thing like that to our Gina."

"Aw, honey. And here Bunny and I were so sure Karaoke Nite was gonna be your lucky charm."

"Not so fast," said Bunny, frowning at Fran. "Douglas McNally didn't lie to Gina. He told her. And he said his marriage was over."

"Just the same," said Gina slowly. "This time, I need to take care of myself. Maybe I should fill out that online dating form, just as you two are always after me to do." She looked up at her friends. "I'm not a young girl who can bounce back easily from these things. I'm a grown woman, I've always taken care of myself, and now I need to use common sense."

"Talk to Theo," declared Bunny. "I haven't known him that long, but there's something about that guy I trust. I bet he'll tell you what you need to know."

"Doug is Theo's best friend," said Gina. "And Theo is very discreet. He's not going to talk about his friend out of school, and I won't ask him to."

"Talk to him," Bunny urged.

Later that day, in fact, Gina had plans to meet Theo. Before Doug left, he had made his choices among all the amazing art pieces Gina and Theo between them had found for him. He had authorized Gina and Theo to make the final decisions, and then Theo had Doug's go-ahead to make the purchases.

"I'll be completely professional and friendly," Gina told herself, "And I won't go all weepy on Theo about Doug. What am I, a middle-schooler?"

As she got ready for her meeting with Theo, Gina kept thinking about Doug. She had come to love those long, lazy mornings they had together, finding some wonderful painting or print or, once, some ceramic pieces, all stunning shape and curve and color. Gina was able to point out their best features to Theo and Doug. She had the know-how. She had the eye. She found herself basking in Doug's admiration.

"I'm getting a real education from you, Gina Prine," he leaned over to her to say one morning.

His nearness was intoxicating. Some very light aftershave tickled her nose. And underneath that, the male scent of him. She was fairly short; she only came up to his broad chest. She almost felt like a child beside him.

He didn't treat her like a child. He treated her like a wise teacher, someone he looked to with respect.

Once, when he brushed her hand with his, seemingly by accident, the effect on her was electric.

Their eyes locked.

Not an accident, Gina thought.

Then back to the hotel lounge. Theo had appointed himself note-taker. He took snapshots of the art, too, with the artists' permission, to remind them all of what they'd seen. The three of them met for coffee every day in the Seaforest's lounge, so they could go over their finds. Often, Doug summoned in a lunch for them.

Every day was perfect. Gina knew these days couldn't last. Doug would be leaving soon, and by now she had discovered that he was a married man. But she savored each day together.

No harm in it, she told herself. I'm the only one who knows how I feel about this, and I'll keep it to myself.

The only morning that wasn't perfect was the morning they drove out to the site of the golf villa. Theo wanted to walk around inside the framed-up walls and get a visual idea about where each of the pieces would go. But when they got there, the real estate agent Doug usually dealt with wasn't there. She was on vacation. In her stead. . .Gina shrank back.

"I'll just wait in the car," she said to Theo.

Silly, to feel that way. The colleague of Doug's real estate agent was Amelia Gardner. Gina didn't particularly want to encounter Amelia. She'd given Amelia's precious JoJo a C, and a generous C at that. But JoJo could do no wrong, as Amelia had let Gina know during several unpleasant parent-teacher conferences over the past year, and Gina doubted Amelia was enough of a professional to keep at least a few snide remarks to herself, even if Gina encountered her with a client.

One of those women who gets a real estate license and then just dabbles in it, thought Gina. Amelia sure didn't have to work for a living. She lived in one of the majestic houses that wound along the shady streets in the best part of town, across the Sound from the beach.

Gina hung back that day and let Doug and Theo deal with Amelia Gardner. When they came back to the car, Doug was shaking his head. "There's something about that woman I just didn't like, Theo," he was saying. "I'll be damned glad when our real gal gets back from vacation."

Theo had rolled his eyes. "Don't call her a gal, bro," he'd said. "Sometimes," Theo said as he exchanged an ironic look with Gina, "I swear you've come out of the age of the dinosaurs, Doug. But about this other one. I agree with you."

Gina bit back a catty remark about Amelia Gardner.

Mostly Gina's mornings with Doug and Theo were magical.

In the afternoons, Gina returned to her house in a daze. She knew she should be starting to work on the jewelry collection she was preparing for the summer craft shows. The first one, on the coast in the quaint town of Southport, was coming right up. Later on, she'd take her pieces to the crafts festivals in the beautiful little mountain communities of the North Carolina Blue Ridge: Maggie Valley, Sapphire Valley. A few over into South Carolina and Georgia. Somehow, she couldn't make herself settle down to work. Being around Doug was too unsettling.

Now those mornings were over. Doug was gone.

So get to work, Gina Prine, she told herself. Chase Douglas McNally out of your mind, because however you feel about him, however he feels about you, he's not available. Maybe he will be, one day. But he's off on his big golf tour, he's a good-looking guy, women probably throw themselves at him, sophisticated women, women with money. And Mrs. McNally might come to her senses. Forget him, Gina.

Now she organized her big sunny workroom with its long farmstead table, and got busy. As she worked, she started feeling more and more serene. The intricate work settled her down, made her feel whole, swept her into a meticulous and beautiful world all her own.

The wires of gold and silver. The little tools. The gemstones, some of them from North Carolina's own mines up in the mountains. The polishing machine. For each piece, Gina had a vision. Then she'd make sketches. Then she'd turn the sketches into beautiful rings. Pendants. Bracelets. Pins. This time she'd planned out a whole series of pieces. A collection unified around a single theme, the Celtic designs that settlers from Scotland and Ireland had brought with them into the North Carolina mountains centuries ago. Their ancestors still treasured them, and these days, so did a lot of other people of many different ancestries. This kind of project required research. Gina reveled in it.

She even regretted that the morning after meeting her friends at The Mermaid, she'd be driving out to see Theo at the golf home site instead of spending the morning in her workroom.

But when she got to the stretch of ground where the condos were being framed up, she was glad. She liked Theo. Liked and respected him.

"Hi, Gina," he said when she got out of her car at the site. "Look at it. Almost finished!"

They stood admiring the villa, one of the first to go up. "Let's go in," said Theo.

They wandered from room to room. In each room, Theo had propped some of their art treasures so they could see where each one would go.

"They're going to look so great," said Gina, her eyes shining. "I'm glad you're here to keep tabs on everything, Theo."

Theo looked uncomfortable. "Uh. About that."

"What?"

"I'm going to have to go back to Chicago. In three days, I'm afraid."

"Oh, no," said Gina. "I'll really miss you, Theo!"

"And I'll miss you. And this." He waved his arms around the golf villa. "Setting this up for Doug has been fun. Well." He drew a breath. "As I think I told you, I don't have to be in Chicago to do my job. Usually. Usually I can do it from my hotel room, with only my laptop."

"You've said that."

"Say one thing for the Seaforest. Tacky as that place is, it has surprisingly good wifi. But now something serious has come up with one of my oldest clients. He lives in Wisconsin, and I need to meet with him personally. I can't do it at long distance. But I can drive over from Chicago, and even if I have to spend a night here and there in Baraboo, I'll be close enough to deal with his crisis personally."

"Baraboo. There's a town named Baraboo?" said Gina, charmed.

"There sure is, and it's a pretty little place. No ocean, I'm afraid. But some lovely lakes nearby."

"Well, then. I'll hope to see you, and Doug too, sometime next year. You'll be back, won't you?"

"Oh, yes," said Theo. "Doug and I, and a few of our other friends from college, visit each other a lot."

"Good," said Gina.

"I'll have to give the key back into the keeping of the real estate agent, though. So this is my last walk-through. I'm thinking it will be best if I lock the art up in Doug's storage area in the club house. That building is finished. The art pieces should all be safe there."

"Good idea," said Gina. "Well, then. Have a good trip back, and I hope to see you again, whenever you come to visit our great little town." She began gathering up her things.

Theo put a hand on her arm. "No, wait. Do you have some time today? Come over to the clubhouse while I supervise the storage, and then have lunch with me. I want you to watch something with me."

"Watch something?"

"On tv. A golf tournament. Doug."

"Oh!" Gina nodded. "Sure, I can do that for a while, but then I'll have to go. I'm working on my collection."

Theo nodded. He knew about Gina's collection. He had visited Gina's workroom. She'd even shown him a few of the pieces in progress.

Theo settled Gina into one of the comfortable leather chairs in the clubhouse Great Room. An enormous screen took up most of one wall. A floor-to-ceiling majestic steel-panel fireplace dominated another. There were groupings of tables and chairs. A bar.

The big doors let out onto a wide brick patio and—not finished yet—landscaping and a pool on the clubhouse grounds.

Theo and Gina were the only ones in the room, except for some workers helping Theo with the careful storage of the art down a corridor past the Great Room. As Theo bustled back and forth, Gina looked around. Very posh, she thought. Kind of cold, though, as if it had been cut out of a catalogue of high-end furnishings. But that was unfair. The place wasn't finished yet.

The resort's brand-new social director came into the room to introduce herself. Laurel Conner. Must be new to town, Gina thought. A little while later, she reappeared to fiddle with the enormous television screen and turn it on and adjust the color and volume.

Eventually Theo sat down beside Gina, and the director reappeared again, a uniformed waitress in tow.

Gina gaped at the waitress. "Ava!" she said, jumping to her feet. Gina and Ava hugged. Then Ava—one of Gina's just-graduated students, handed menus to Theo and Gina.

This is my new job," Ava told Gina. To Theo, she said, "Ms. Prine was my art teacher. I'm an artist, thanks to her—"

"A good one, too," Gina put in.

"—but you know us art people. We have to have our day jobs."

"I do indeed," said Theo. He and Gina gave Ava their lunch orders. Not too long after, Ava reappeared and set them up at a little table positioned just in front of the enormous screen.

Gina took a bite of her roast beef sandwich and reached for a chip. She settled herself in for a boring hour or two before she could gracefully excuse herself and get back to her workroom. She didn't know much about golf. Once, she and Theo had watched a tournament Doug was playing in. But he was far down the roster of players. He didn't come in last, but down there with the last-comers. No tv crew followed him about the course.

Gina had taken in as much as she could as Theo explained the game to her.

And now. . . Gina thought to herself, watching. The little white ball. . .is rolling toward. . . the little hole. . .

It was all very slow. The voices of the announcers were hushed, as if they were in church. The Church of Golf. The smattering of applause from the watching crowds seemed excessively polite.

Theo was pumped, though, and by the end of the tournament, or as much of it as Gina could get herself to watch, she thought she understood a bit more about what made the game so absorbing and exciting to its fans. Theo was a good teacher.

"Do you play?" Gina had asked him.

"Sometimes. I'm a real duffer. I'd never play with Doug, not even for fun." Theo rolled his eyes. "Thanks to years of watching Doug, and one of our other college roommates, I'm a big fan of the game, though."

"Another roommate was a golfer," said Gina.

"Yeah. Stevie. He wasn't all that serious about it. He was on the golf team in college, but not a standout, like Doug. He plays great recreational golf, though. I wouldn't dream of playing with him, either. Every one of them was a jock, except me, the theater nerd. One of our roommates was a quarterback on the football team, second stringer. Two were on the baseball team. One of those guys even made it to the minors."

"A lot of roommates. A lot of sports."

"Yeah. I guess you'd call them housemates, actually. We all pledged the same fraternity, and then we all lived off-campus in the same funky house. Good times. Even though I was the only non-jock, we all got along great. Mostly. There was Cody. Very devout in a very rigid religious tradition. He wanted the best for me, that guy. Tried to pray the gay away, but it didn't work." Theo snickered. "Still in touch with all of them, even Cody. Well. Not one of them. Poor Salazar, he died young."

"Ha," said Gina, imagining Doug as a young frat-boy jock, and how very different her own college experience had been, commuting to college, scrapping for the money to keep going, semester by semester. "Sounds like Doug comes from a privileged background," she said only.

"You could say that. Some of us in the house were scholarship guys. Athletic scholarships. Doug's family was pretty well-off."

"What about yours?"

"Mother's a doctor. Father's a doctor," said Theo.

"Wow. Still living?"

"Amazing, yeah. Both in their nineties, both still going strong. Retired. They used to travel a lot. Now they're slowing down."

"And you're from Chicago?"

"Yep. Skokie, actually."

"And Doug?"

"Doug grew up all around. His dad was one of these corporate guys who moves his family every couple years as he climbs the corporate ladder."

Gina wanted to find out about Doug. All about Doug. But she didn't want to sound too eager. "Parents still alive too?"

"His old dad is. That man will never die. We had to stick him in a nursing home last year, and he was not pleased. To put it mildly. Mrs. McNally died a few years back. Went to her rest, as they say. Man, did she need a rest."

"Doug's father sounds like a challenge," said Gina, grinning.

"Doug's dad is a piece of work." Theo shook his head. "One of the reasons Doug settled here is so he could check on his dad. Nursing home's up in Raleigh."

"Ah. I see," said Gina.

"What about you, Gina?"

"My parents are both dead. Died pretty young. I've been on my own since my late teens."

"No sisters or brothers?"

"None."

Theo was about to reply. But instead he lunged for the remote and turned up the volume. "Hey. Here's the tournament coverage."

"Is this going to be a good one?" said Gina politely.

"It's a big one, one of the majors. Important," he explained.

"Maybe we'll catch sight of a tiny Doug behind some trees," she said.

Theo looked over at her and laughed.

The last time they did this, they thought maybe they'd caught a glimpse of him striding down the fairway, but the video shot was so far away, and he was so in the background, that they weren't sure.

"Gina. This is a three-day tournament. The coverage on tv has been great, and not just on the Golf Channel. Guess who's on the leader board? Guess who you are about to see, as huge as that wall over there?"

"Doug?" said Gina, amazed.

"Doug," said Theo, and as he said it, Doug himself came into view, vast and gorgeous, his tall, fit body, the flash of his smile.

". . . the phenom of this tournament, Douglas McNally," the announcer was saying. His partner nodding grave agreement. The camera had switched from the shot of Doug to the head shots of the commentators on some studio set.

"Right you are, Phil," said the other announcer. "Douglas McNally, from the back of the pack. McNally hasn't been doing all that well, but I'd say in this outing he's playing out of his mind, Phil."

"You know, Ron," said the first announcer. "Douglas McNally is one of the oldest players still on the Tour."

"In his heyday years, he was quite the player, Phil," said Ron. "Never won a major, but he sure came close."

"You are absolutely right, Ron. And look at him today. He's back, Ron. Douglas McNally is back!"

Theo let out a whoop. With embarrassment, Gina realized she had, too. The two of them looked at each other and laughed.

"Doug says this is his last year on the Tour," Theo told her. "Guess he plans to go out in a blaze of glory."

Gina had never known golf to be a white-knuckle experience, not even after Theo explained the game to her. Not even when she knew she was watching a tournament where Doug was in it, even though he was one of the struggling players counted out by all the announcers.

Now she gripped the arms of her club chair so tightly that, wow, her knuckles really were turning white. A white-knuckle experience. That old expression was simply true.

Gina stayed there all afternoon, watching. Watching for a glimpse of Doug. And there were many.

By the end of the afternoon, the club director had come in, too. "That's Mr. McNally," she said, her voice amazed. "Our Mr. McNally."

"Sure is," said Theo.

"I knew some of the fellows told me he's a great golfer, but wow."

Theo and Gina exchanged triumphant looks. Our Mr. McNally. Ours.

At one point, Doug was third on the leader board. Then he began to fade.

"Awww," said Gina.

"Nope, don't say that, Gina. Doug is playing great golf."

"Ron and Phil, they're predicting those other two guys will duel it out for the win."

"Yeah. That's probably what will happen, although in golf, as I've come to find out," said Theo, "anything can happen."

Doug finished fifth.

"Gina, that's great," said Theo. "Doug just made a lot of money, and he got a lot of attention and respect, too."

Gina nodded. The television commentators were confirming it. The winner got a big interview, the guy who came in second got one. And Doug got one.

"Douglas McNally," said one of the commentators to Doug, appearing with him behind the commentators' podium. "The Cinderella Man of this tournament."

Doug grinned.

Gina wanted to rush the podium, right through the screen, and hug him.

"How are you feeling right now?" said the other commentator.

"Real good, Ron," said Doug. "I played the game I hoped I could play. You never know. Weather. Chance. All those things. A bit of bad luck there at the end, with the bogeys. But I'm happy."

"He looks happy," said Gina to Theo.

"Yeah," said Theo.

That's when Gina noticed something. She knew her own eyes must be shining. But Theo's eyes were shining, too.

That's not friendship, thought Gina. That's love.

Theo turned to say something and caught Gina looking at him. He shrugged, his expression rueful. "I've always had a thing for Doug," he said softly. "From freshman year in college. Nothing I can do about it. Doug's made one way, I'm made another."

Gina grabbed Theo's hand and squeezed it. "But you can be his good friend."

"And I am," said Theo.

"Aren't you a little worried—" Gina began.

"Nah," said Theo. "Doug is thick as bricks. He'll never know. And you won't tell."

"Of course not," said Gina.

"But Gina," said Theo, looking her in the eye. "What are you going to do about Doug."

"What do you mean, what am I going to do about Doug?" Gina was taken aback.

"Just what I said. Doug is thick as bricks. You're not. What are you going to do?"

Gina shook her head. "He's a married man, Theo."

"Not for long."

"You don't know that for sure," said Gina. She made herself take a lighter tone. "Well, Theo. This has been great. I'm so happy for Doug. And the art is safely packed away, and you're headed for Chicago. I'm going to really miss you. Come back soon. And now I need to get myself to my workroom."

"And your art."

"Yes, Theo. And my art."

"It saves you, Gina. I've noticed that. It's your refuge."

"I suppose it does," said Gina.

Later, closing the door to her workroom and settling to her tasks, she knew it did.

Pompom misses you

DOUG THREW HIMSELF in a happy daze across the king-sized bed in his posh hotel room. He supposed he should have economized. He'd had a funny feeling about this tournament, though. It was the last big one.

So he had treated himself.

No more. From now on, he'd be extra prudent. One part of him wanted to exult, with Ron the Commentator, "Douglas McNally's back!" But the other part of him, the sensible part, grinned at him and said only, "Douglas McNally's old."

Not old, he argued with himself. I'm as fit as I ever was. Fitter, to be honest, because I've cut back on all the wining and dining. But that other, sensible part, still grinning: You know what I mean, Dougie.

Yeah, he did. Too old for competitive golf. All the young guys had the power moves. The power swings. He couldn't do those things any longer, the grandstanding of his young manhood. You're right, he told this sensible self. As the Tour wound down, he'd probably fall back into the company of the last guys on the board again, statistics being what they are. And then, if he lost his card, this time he wouldn't fight it. He'd go away gracefully. If he didn't lose it this time? Well. He was sure to lose it the next year. He'd just keep playing and collecting his paycheck until he couldn't any more. That's all. He fixed his sensible self with a stern look.

"I'm admitting it. You're right. But don't call me Dougie," he growled. Rolled his eyes at himself when he realized he'd said it out loud.

As he lay in that glow, another feeling was making itself insistently felt. Thinking about Gina. About the softness of her skin, the few times they'd touched. He hardened at the thought.

A knock on his hotel room door interrupted his private little celebration. His erection wilted.

"Ugh," he said, swinging to his feet, hopping back into his pants, which he had shucked off. He cracked the door.

"Room service."

"Uh. I didn't—"

"Says it's a gift from your best fan," said the bellhop, reading a small white envelope.

Doug pulled the door open wide, mystified.

In creaked the little cart. On it wobbled a bottle of champagne, tucked into a silver bucket filled with ice shavings.

Doug tipped the bellhop and sat on the bed, staring at the bucket and wondering. There was a single flute, so not from anyone expecting to join him. Well, he told himself. There was the card, sticking up jauntily from the bucket. Let's see.

He reached over and took the envelope, which read, just as the bellhop had said, "From your best fan." Doug opened the envelope and looked at the card inside. Lay back on the bed, groaning.

Hey, Dougie, lover-man! Congrats on a fantastic day. We've had our problems. Let's take a mulligan, okay, sweetie? Come home to Charlotte as soon as the Tour is over. Pompom misses you, and so do I. Kisses, Jaclin.—heart emoji—*Your best fan.*

"Not gonna work. Not this time." She'd tried similar tactics before. This time he'd been sure she was as ready for divorce as he was.

Didn't matter. He was divorcing her. She was false, through and through. He didn't care how much it cost to get rid of her. And she knew that, damn her.

He thought about it. When she saw he came out in the big money just now, she probably concocted her mulligan plan on the spot.

Even Jaclin should be able to see it, though. Fantastic day of golf or not, even Jaclin should realize that Doug was too old for competitive golf. Jaclin, he thought, is cunning. But she's not very bright.

As for Pompom. "Pompom misses me," Teeth gritted, he looked at the card again. "I'll just bet he does."

Luckily, the Tour had months to go.

He decided he wouldn't reply to her pathetic overture. He pulled a shirt on and walked the champagne barefoot down to the hotel's common room, where several fans and several golfers he knew waved at him and called out congratulations.

"Hey, everyone. Someone sent me a nice bottle of champagne. Hate for it to go to waste. I'm on the wagon. I'll put it out in here for anyone who wants some." Then he tipped one of the hotel's employees to send over glasses, and went back to his room to go to bed.

He couldn't sleep, though. He tossed and turned. Funny thing of it was, he could think of only one thing. Person, that is.

Gina Prine.

He tried getting himself off on thoughts of her. It worked. Kind of. But he craved the real Gina.

Now aren't you the funny one, he scolded himself. He'd always dated the blonde sorority queen-bees in college, and the cheerleader types.

True, his disastrous first marriage hadn't been to a woman like that. He'd really blown that one. Tressa was a lovely person. He'd married her just as he'd begun his pro golf career. Their marriage had ended badly, and he knew it was his fault.

He twisted away in pain from the thoughts his first marriage provoked in him. Tressa had died several years back. Cancer. A shame. She hadn't deserved it. She hadn't deserved him, the conceited ass that he was. He turned these thoughts off. He'd gotten good at doing that. Like a light switch. Off.

Anyway.

You'd think after Tressa he would have learned his lesson about the consequences of being an arrogant hound. But noooo. Some of his fellow pros had served up their most notorious groupie, Jaclin, on a platter, practically. And he had been foolish enough to fall for it, and for those huge blue eyes, and those perky breasts. . .

If there was a woman who was the opposite of all that, it must be Gina Prine. She was smart. She was pretty. But she was an artist, for chrissakes. Who dated an artist? And she was around his own age. Must be. Wasn't there some Dougie McNally Law enacted, mandating he had to have a woman at least ten years younger than himself?

Gina's breasts, though. He'd caught himself hungrily eyeing her, especially that day she'd worn that tee emphasizing her curves. They weren't as out there and aggressive as Jaclin's boobs. They hadn't had work, for one. Jaclin's sure had. They were hard as rocks. But Gina's breasts. He swallowed hard. They were fine, and the time he'd pressed against her, he felt how round and soft they were.

If only Theo was around. Theo would talk sense to Doug.

He thought again of Gina. She was little, but she was strong. The planes of her face were strong, and she knew who she was. She didn't need some man, especially not a two-time loser like Doug. Especially not some washed-up jock.

Doug lay alone in his opulent hotel room and longed for her. He wondered what she would feel like, if he put his hands on her. If he peeled away the armor of her clothes. He was starting to get hard again at the thought of her.

Nah. It was impossible. She'd never want someone like him. She'd want some cultured guy. Somebody as whip-smart as she was.

Doug turned on the television. Then he turned it off. Nothing but junk. And replays of the tournament. Before he clicked the off button he got a glimpse of himself, smiling fatuously. Ron, or maybe it was Phil, was smiling fatuously back.

OFF.

His hand stole out to the nightstand. Felt for his reading glasses. Pretty soon all of his self-hatred was far away from him. He was deep into a book, Mary Beard's *SPQR*. Funny. He'd hated history as a student. He hadn't even liked reading much, and he still didn't like fiction. History, now. It had become his only solace. His drug of choice, and schlocky fare like the History Channel wasn't good enough. He read every kind of history he could get his hands on, from every era. Every culture.

Bring it on. He might be a petty, pathetic person at the end of a petty, pathetic career. But the world was full of amazing events and people and places, and he wanted to visit them all, if only in his mind.

The book he was reading couldn't banish Gina Prine from his inner eye, though. Or the ache for her from his body. But it could distract him.

He fell asleep reading, his glasses askew, the book flopped across his chest.

Road trip

IT WAS A RELIEF TO get on the road, Gina thought, pulling out of her driveway and pointing her old Ford down the first of the little two-lane highways that would lead her meandering from Currituck Cove to Southport. She decided to spend four or five hours on the road with a break for lunch at oh, maybe Kinston.

Gina didn't love driving when she was in a hurry to get somewhere. She loved it when she could take her time, stop off at a roadside stand selling homegrown tomatoes or summer squash, maybe take a side-trip to a little tearoom if she got tired and needed a break.

A high-end farmer's market along her route had encouraged her, last year, to bring some of her jewelry by. When she reached the little place, she stopped. The market had a case where she could sell her pieces on consignment. The market had some interesting local art for sale on its walls, too—a good sign. She thought she might give their consignment case a try. She left a few pieces with the manager, who ooed and ahhed over them. She waved and got back in the Ford. On the way back, she'd stop again to see if they'd sold. And then she could get herself some flowers for home. They stood in colorful bunches under a striped awning. Makes me wish I were a painter, she thought. A good one, anyway.

Driving down the highway, she sang. Except when she caught herself singing *Total Eclipse of the Heart*.

Stop, she said to herself softly. Just stop thinking about him. If you don't, you're gonna get hurt. Doug McNally had lived a completely different life from her own, a prosperous life, even from childhood, and he was a jock. Worst of all, she reminded herself, he was married.

She and he had nothing in common. "Nothing," Gina said out loud. She drove on.

What with all the puttering she had done along the way, it was late afternoon when Gina pulled into Southport. Gina loved Southport. It was a very different kind of beach town from Currituck Cove. Artsy, quaint in a good (not run-down) way, close enough to Wilmington to have more of a big-town experience if you needed one, a lot of fun historic sites, and quite a few nearby affluent beach communities stuffed with shoppers eager for craft shows to browse and one-of-a-kind jewelry to buy. Gina always had some of her most profitable craft show days in Southport.

When she was there, she always stayed at the same place, a cozy B&B near the fire station, right off the water.

They knew her there. When she checked in, Mrs. Fussell was in the front parlor to greet her. "Dear Gina! Don't you look marvelous," she crooned.

Gina felt good about that. Before she left, Fran and Bunny had shepherded her back to Johanna the stylist in Norfolk. This time Gina had paid, paid quite a bit. But the results were worth it.

Doggedly over the last months, Bunny had insisted on giving Gina makeup lessons. Now Gina owned a full complement of Adorable Me cosmetics and knew how to apply them without looking painted up and fake.

"Shouldn't she. . ." Fran had hesitated. "What about Adorée instead of Adorable Me, or that other high-end stuff you're starting to sell. Mélisande."

Bunny winked. "Guess what?" she stage-whispered. "It's the same stuff, just different packaging and marketing."

So Gina was pretty confident she really was looking her best.

"Looka here." Mrs. Fussell stepped back to reveal an enormous vase of roses. There was a card. Mrs. Fussell handed it to Gina.

Welcome back to Southport! the card read. *Dinner Sunday? Archer.*

"Awww, that nice man," said Gina.

Mrs. Fussell nodded, beaming. Clearly, she'd snooped and read the card, but Gina could see it wouldn't have even occurred to her not to. "I do believe he's sweet on you, Miss Gina," she said.

"Oh," said Gina with a laugh. "He's just, you know, being Archer." Archer Deveraux. Southport gallery owner. He had some of Gina's things on consignment, too.

Actually, Archer's main gallery was in Charlotte, with a big branch in Wilmington, and his beach-branch, as he called it, in Southport. Gina's jewelry was at the Southport gallery. She aspired to get them into the Charlotte gallery too, or at the least, placed at the Wilmington gallery. Archer sending her flowers. That was a good sign.

Archer lived just outside Southport, in a big white-columned house inland, down a lane of trees draped in Spanish moss. He was quite a bit older than Gina, acted a lot younger, courtly, Southern, a widower.

When she got to her room and unlocked her phone, there was a text from Archer with the same invitation. *Dinner Sunday?* Sunday was the last day of the craft fair. Gina would leave Monday morning.

"Sure," she texted back. "Looking forward to it."

"I'll see you tomorrow at the opening—ttyl" was his reply.

Gina dressed casually for the first day of the craft fair. It would be a long, grueling experience, and the sun was hot. Sleeveless tucked white shirt. Light gray linen clamdiggers. Sturdy white keds. A broad straw hat.

Right after a great breakfast of Mrs. Fussell's eggs, biscuits, and gravy, she strolled from Mrs. Fussell's place down to the park where the craft show was setting up, drawing her rolling bin of jewelry and supplies and signage after her. She found her own white tent and began working on the table and arranging her displays. At last, satisfied, she strung her sign from the front of her tent: *Gina Prine, Jewelry*, was all it said, in a distinctive font with soft intertwined floating colors in the background. This year, she'd thought about making a Celtic knot logo, at least for this collection, but she decided she didn't want her signage to pin her down to just one type of customer and style. She laid out brochures and business cards. Then she opened up one of the show's folding chairs and sat down to wait.

She did not have to wait long. Pretty soon, she found she'd been on her feet without a break for an hour and a half. So far, the take was very satisfying, she thought, looking over at her cash box. Although she conducted more and more of her business these days through a credit card reader attached to her phone, or a payment app.

Whether they bought or not, a lot of shoppers walked away with her brochure, her business card, or both. She was glad she had gotten plenty of them printed up. She'd learned from her mistakes a few years ago, when she had printed too few.

"Look at you!" boomed a voice behind her.

Gina spun around. "Archer!"

Archer swept her off her feet and gave her a smacking kiss on each cheek. He set her carefully back down. "You are a vision, Gina Prine. I love the new look."

"You're looking pretty great yourself, Archer." And he was. He was a vigorous older man, dressed in white linen sharply-creased trousers, pink linen shirt with the sleeves rolled up, his thick snow-white hair drawn back low into a man ponytail.

A tat up the inside of his left arm read, "Fear no art!"

"Hey, I see you are swamped. Find me at closing in the beer tent." He waved and moved on.

Later that day, flushed with success, Gina packed up. She rolled her cart to the beer tent. Archer waved her over, and she slid onto the bench beside him.

"Thanks for the roses, Archer," said Gina. "What a nice gesture."

"I need to treat my best designers right," he said, smiling at her over his pint glass. "Don't want them going to the competition on me."

After they'd engaged in some small talk, Archer got straight to the point. "Look, Gina. I nearly sent you a note with this month's check from the gallery, but then I thought, hell, no, I'm seeing the lovely lady in person in only a few days, and I'll tell her then." Archer handed her a fat envelope. "The check. And the note."

She tucked it in with the cash box in her cart. "Don't leave me in suspense, Archer. Tell me what the note says."

"It says you're my top earner in your category, Gina. It says why don't we make arrangements for you to show your stuff in my Wilmington gallery, too."

"Why not Charlotte," said Gina.

Archer looked at her levelly. "Why not."

They shook on it.

"When can I have product?" he asked.

"As soon as I get back from this, I'll get some over to Wilmington. And. . .Charlotte?"

"Yeah. And Charlotte," he said.

"I'm headed to the big craft fairs in the mountains next," she told him. "So after that, I should have time to make more for you."

"That's fine. I think I'll sell all you can get me. I took a look around at your new collection while I was in your tent. Looks like it's gonna be very popular. Looks like it already is."

"I sold a bunch and got a bunch of orders," Gina said, pleased.

"You're gonna be a busy lady once you get home."

When Gina rose to go, he stopped her. "Look. Let me walk you back to Mrs. Fussell's. I know it's high summer, and still daylight, and I know this is a wonderful little town, and very safe. But you're walking through the streets of town with a cashbox, Miss Gina. Need to be careful."

Gina's first impulse was to laugh at his Southern courtliness. Then she thought better of it. He was right. "Okay," she said.

While they walked, he gave her a big lecture on safety and business practices. "You're not some little crafter lady any longer, Gina, if you ever were. You're an artist. And you're a businesswoman. Gotta start acting like one."

"What do you suggest?"

"Well, you're through here often enough. I'd say open an account at one of the bigger banks, one with branches up in your area, over in the mountains, all over. Then deposit your earnings at the end of every day. And I can deposit your checks from the galleries directly there, too."

"You're right, Archer," she admitted. "I'll do it tomorrow on my break."

"Thatta girl," he said. He approved of her card reader, too, and connection with the most popular apps.

His patronizing attitude annoyed her. But dammit, he was right. She did need to start thinking of herself as the owner of a business, not just an artist.

And right then, she realized she knew the very person to talk to about all that. Bunny Dowdy. And Fran. Fran with her banking experience.

Gina had her crew. And they had her back. They always did. They always had.

Big idea

DOUG'S MANAGER PAUL called him with a big idea. Golf in England. "There are a few nice low-key tournaments in Cornwall and Devon this year. You should fly over there and play. These are lesser known than the big courses in Scotland and so forth. But give yourself a little vacation. You deserve it. The scenery is magnificent."

Doug knew what Paul was trying to tell him. Kick back a little. Get yourself a little prize money, play in a beautiful setting, ease yourself into retirement. Don't go for anything too taxing.

After the big splash he'd made, and at one of the majors, too, Doug's game had predictably gone downhill. He was finishing at the very bottom more often than not, and when he wasn't, he found himself in the bottom middle of the pack. He just didn't have the strength he'd had as a young golfer.

And no one expects me to, he thought. I don't expect me to. So why does it sting so much?

England did sound nice. He signed on, got his travel papers in order, and went over.

The experience was glorious, and also chastening.

Glorious because of the beautiful links courses with their amazing sweep of fairways; in Cornwall, often to the top of the stunning sea cliffs.

Chastening, because his manager's sunny predictions—kick back, get some easy prize money—were 'way overblown. The courses were challenging—links golf had never been his strong point, anyhow—and the competition, superb. There Doug was again, at the back of the pack.

He sort of didn't care. He worried about his lack of humiliation over each fresh demonstration that he was over the hill. He should be eating his liver over every mistake. Every bogey. Every missed putt. He wasn't. Didn't that as good as set him up for failure? But no, it actually made his game more relaxed, and he began playing a little better. Not well enough. "I'll probably lose my card right here," he thought. And the thought did not scare him.

Wisely, he'd chosen not to stay in an expensive hotel. He'd put up in a lovely guest house overlooking the harbor in Plymouth, which gave him a central location from which to travel to any of the courses in Cornwall and Devon with a minimum of time on the road.

Best of all, his host was a history buff, full of knowledge about the region, from prehistory through the World War II era. And of course, Doug being a Yank, he told Doug all about the departure of the Mayflower to New England from Plymouth Harbor.

On his off-days, Doug poked around historical sites.

He decided the Roman era fascinated him most.

"Did you know the Romans called the British Isles the Cassiterides? The Tin Isles. We were the world's leading source of tin for the ancient world. Right here. Cornwall and Devon have some of the largest tin deposits in the world, and the Romans found them," said his host.

"Tin, huh," said Doug.

"Very, very important to their economy, those old Roman blokes." At Doug's look, he elaborated. "You have to have tin to smelt bronze. And those people needed a lot of bronze. Course, bronze needs copper, too. And we have the copper mines around here as well. Even with the advent of the Iron Age, even with the coming of steel, bronze was still in demand. And those Romans, you know they had invented plumbing and water delivery systems. Their pipes needed tin for soldering."

"Wow," said Doug. "Tin. Who knew."

"You can go out to see some old tin mines if you're really interested."

Doug took an entire day to go down to a quaint Cornish seaside village where ancient tin ingots had been found. There was nothing much to see, tin-wise, but the beach was lovely. It made Doug homesick for his own beach. Currituck Cove.

And it's really not even MY beach, thought Doug. Not even really home.

But it's going to be, and in only a few months, that inside voice told him. He had to tell it to shut up, then, because once he started thinking about Currituck Cove, he started thinking about Gina. And I can't, he told himself. I shouldn't.

Strange, then. His mind wandered to Tressa, his first wife. She'd been a Brit, come over to the US on a student exchange. Doug had met her in college. He'd been smitten by her fragile beauty and that lush accent.

As he walked the sands, Doug thought about her for the first time in quite a while. Really thought about her. She was from around here somewhere. Silly of him. He'd forgotten exactly where. Their marriage hadn't lasted very long. He hadn't done anything overt to alienate her. But his career had just gotten started. Later, he realized he'd simply ignored her. One day he got back from the gru-eling weeks scrapping to get his tour card on the Korn Ferry Tour, to find a note from her. Just "I'm leaving and going home."

Thank god no children were involved.

A few years ago, he'd heard by indirect means, an acquaintance from college who had known her, that she'd died. Sad. He'd lost touch with her, with her parents, long ago. He supposed by now her parents must be dead, too. He closed his eyes, letting the sea breeze riffle over him, and hoped she'd had a good life. Why hadn't he found out? Why hadn't he kept up? He felt his shortcomings as a person keenly.

A lunch of traditional Cornish pasties in the village cheered him up. Now he wandered the little streets toward the car park.

Before he got back to his car, a small sign caught his eye. TIN MUSEUM, it read. On an impulse, he went over to the weathered house with the sign and peered in through some dim windows. The place seemed closed. Maybe too late in the day.

He was turning away when the door burst open. Standing in the doorway, a large, beaming woman in a brown jumper (their word for "sweater," he reminded himself), big brown brogans, and thick stockings rolled down about her ankles.

"Come to the museum? We're open!"

Doug hesitated, about to say he'd changed his mind, he didn't have time. Instead, he went in.

It was, as he suspected, a small place with not much to see. All the exhibits looked handmade.

But the more he poked around, the more fascinated he became. The exhibits told him mostly about tin mining in the seventeenth, eighteenth, nineteenth centuries. There were exhibits of old min-ers' implements. A whole exhibit about that regional delicacy, the pasty, a meat pie made to fit into the hand. The pasties looked like little half-moons, one side crimped all around.

"Ye never eat the crust," the museum owner told him, hovering at his elbow. He was her only visitor. She owned the little place, he discovered. "The miners took pasties into the mines for lunch. Their womenfolk made them special, and the miners held them by the crimped crusts and bit into them. Then they always threw the crusts away. It's because of the arsenic. The earth of the mines was full of it, and it would dirty the hands of the miners, and if they ate the crusts of the pasty, where their dirty hands had been holding them, why, they'd poison themselves, you know."

Doug did know. At lunch, realizing he was from the States, the lunchroom owner had told him the same tale. But he nodded along politely as he heard it all again from the tin museum lady.

"Beef. Potato. Swedes. That's all there is in a pasty," the lunchroom owner had said, as she handed him his plate. She taught him how to say it, too. "Not PAY-stee or PAH-stee," she said. "It's PAST-stee." And how to tell whether a pasty was real and not fake. "If that's not the filling, the beef, the potatoes, the swedes, it's not a true pasty. And them in Devon crimp it wrong."

Swedes, he thought. Rutabaga. So that's what those vegetables were. If you'd asked him, how about a big helping of rutabaga for lunch, he'd have said no thank you. But the pasties were delicious.

He was amused by the insistence on what was Cornish and what Devonian. Like whether you put the strawberry jam on the scone first, or the clotted cream, in a cream tea.

Now the tin museum lady steered him over to an exhibit that really did thrill him. It was a handmade poster, as they all were. But affixed to it was a newspaper article just beginning to yellow.

"A few years back, the archaeologist fellows were all over this coast. They found the wreck of an ancient ship, just ruins, you know, and in it the traces of tin ingots. Solved a big mystery. People around here, we've always thought we were the Tin Isles that the Romans talked about. You know about the Tin Isles and the Romans?"

Doug nodded that he did.

"Well, some thought the Tin Isles might be off the coast of Spain or some completely different place. But the archaeologists solved the mystery. Us! We're the Tin Isles."

Doug took a picture of the newspaper article with his cell.

The woman was plucking at his sleeve. "And look at these."

She led him to a glass case. Under the glass were amazing crystals. Some were almost black, others yellowish.

"Cassiterite. The ore."

"They're very pretty."

"There are some can make very pretty rings and things out of cassiterite."

Doug's eyes opened wide. "You don't know where I can get some cassiterite, do you?"

The woman gave him a smug look and led him to her counter, where bins held souvenir cassiterite crystals for purchase.

Doug bought an entire scoop of them. He'd bet Gina had never thought about cassiterite as a gemstone.

Back at the guest house, he was ashamed of himself. Gina would probably laugh at him, and besides, he shouldn't be bringing her little gifts. But he tucked the sack of crystals in with his luggage. I mean, he owed her a thank you for all the art advice and the art field trips, didn't he?

She could set them in copper! Jewelry evoking Ancient Rome!

What a dork, he thought to himself. Getting all excited about something like that. What a big idea, he jeered at himself. Gina would just laugh at him.

Think about something else, he demanded of himself when he found himself, as usual, getting hot and hard at the very thought of her.

Don't think about her. You're not allowed to.

Meet not-so-cute

AT THE END OF HER RUN at Southport, Gina packed up, leaving only a few things out to change into the next morning, for her drive back to Currituck Cove. For her dinner with Archer, she put on a cool, understated bisque seersucker dress she had bought at a chic Southport shop that sold only natural fibers.

And I paid too much for it, she thought, pulling it over her head with satisfaction. Wait'll Bunny and Fran see this.

Archer greeted her, helping her from her car with both hands outstretched. He air-kissed her cheek and led her up the wide stairs to his wraparound porch, its beadboard ceiling a beautiful haint blue, and into the tall shady front hall of his house. A hundred years old if it's a day, thought Gina, looking around. Maybe older. And in great shape, too.

"I've got our dinner going, darlin. Come on out to the kitchen with me," he said.

The kitchen, like the rest of the house, was outsized and a delightful contradiction, the original flagstones on the floor, gleaming modern appliances filling the space with stainless steel almost to the rough beams of the building's high-ceilinged original structure.

Archer equipped Gina with a chilled glass of white wine. As he finished with the cooking, he dipped up sauces for her to taste, popped a shrimp into her mouth, and fed her anecdote after fascinating anecdote about artists he knew, art he had sold, celebrities he had met. It would have sounded like boasting in another man. Out of Archer's mouth, with his soft patrician accent, it was charming.

Archer was a great cook. The evening was magical. At the end of it, as Archer was trying to persuade Gina to have another glass of wine and she was demurring, needing to drive back to Mrs. Fussell's and make an early departure in the morning, he dropped his bombshell on her.

"Gina," he said, his eyes soft. "I have a proposal for you."

"What's that?" Gina said, thinking about his Charlotte gallery and some interesting new business idea.

"No," he said, fixing her with a look "A proposal, Gina."

Her hand flew to her mouth.

"I'm asking you to marry me, Gina."

Later, tossing and turning in Mrs. Fussell's comfortable much too flossy bed, Gina thought it over. She'd had to say no.

"Take some time, Gina," he urged. "Think it over. We make a great team."

Why did you say no? she asked herself. Because she didn't love him? Yes, of course that was it. But he was right, wasn't he? They did make a great team. At their age, friendship and compatibility were more important than love. So what had stopped her?

She knew what.

And it made no sense.

Her heart was already claimed, and by a man she couldn't have. By a man who probably didn't even know he had claimed it. Doug.

She drove home a troubled woman. All night, instead of thinking about Archer, she thought of Doug. And her thoughts led her to a longing so physical she hardly slept at all.

Now, on the road home, she didn't even stop to see how her consignment pieces had done at the farmer's market, or buy the flowers.

Her roses from Archer were still fresh. Mrs. Fussell had tried to wrap them in newspaper for her to take back with her.

"No, Mrs. Fussell. You keep them. They're so pretty, and they may wilt in the car."

"Oh, honey," said Mrs. Fussell, putting a hand on her arm and giving her a pitying smile. Mrs. Fussell had the uncanny knack, it seemed, of seeing right through Gina.

Why is it I'm surrounded by mind-readers? Gina thought fretfully. Am I really that transparent?

When she got home, all she wanted to do was make herself an early dinner and go to bed.

That was not to be.

She walked in her front door to the ringing of her phone. She tried answering it, tucking it under her chin while she fished for her housekeys.

"'Lo?"

"Ms. Prine?"

"Yes?"

Oh, hell, thought Gina. A telemarketer. She hadn't managed to get a look at the screen as she'd answered, and she didn't recognize the voice.

"It's Laurel Conner. From the club."

Club? thought Gina blankly.

"The Currituck Cove Golf Club."

Ohhh. "Oh, hello, Ms. Conner. What can I do for you."

Laurel Conner sounded a bit frazzled. "I wasn't sure who to call about this. Mr. McNally isn't back yet, and Mr. Greene had to leave. So the realtor suggested you might be able to help."

"Is anything wrong?"

"I'm not sure. It's about the art."

"Oh, yes. Theo packed it up in Doug's storage room. I hope nothing has happened to it."

"Not exactly."

Now Gina was alarmed.

"It's Mrs. McNally," Laurel Conner went on. "She says she doesn't like it. She told me to clear it out of the storage room."

"What?" Gina made herself calm down. Mrs. McNally. Doug's wife. "Okay," she said, taking a deep breath. "And is Mrs. McNally there now?"

"Yes. She's here with the realtor. She's insisting I get rid of it. But I can't just put it out on the street. I can't just dump it. I tried getting in touch with Mr. McNally, but his manager says he's out of the country."

Gina thought fast. "Would you like me to come by and pick it up? I can keep it safe at my house, and then when Doug—Mr. Mc-Nally—comes back, he can let me know what to do with it. Oh, and I have Theo's phone number. He'll know what to do. Actually, he's the best person to deal with this, not me."

"Could you call him? That would be great," said Laurel. "I don't have a number for him. In the meantime, though, uh—I think you better come over here."

"I'll be right there. Thank you for calling, Laurel."

Gina clicked off, trembling. She did have to get over there. All that art. Thousands of dollars' worth, and it was all great stuff. Each piece somebody's dream. She couldn't risk it getting damaged, any more than Laurel Conner could. Gina wouldn't be able to live with herself if even a single piece was ruined.

But she also knew she had no business going over there and getting in the middle of some conflict between Douglas McNally and his wife. She knew that for certain, as surely as she knew she couldn't abandon the art.

She fumbled through her contact list. There. There was Theo's number. She rang. He didn't pick up.

She left a message. "Theo, this is Gina Prine. Something urgent has come up. Doug's wife is here, and apparently she wants to dump all Doug's art. I don't know what to do. Nobody can get in touch with Doug. Call me. I could use some advice!"

She rushed back to her car and got in. Drove to the golf club, trying her mightiest not to get distracted by the flood of panicky feelings that threatened to overwhelm her.

High summer, and it was still light. She pulled into the golf club parking lot, registering somewhere in the back of her mind that the club construction was almost complete.

At the far end of the parking lot, she could see three little figures. One of them was obviously agitated. Gesticulating. As she neared, she could hear raised voices.

She really didn't want to take a step further toward them. She really did want to head back to her car, go home, and pretend the insanity of this situation wasn't happening.

But it was.

She shouldn't be involved in it, whatever it turned out to be.

But she was.

She gave herself a little shake and moved in toward the group, three women.

One of them was Laurel Conner. One, a woman she'd never seen before, very well-dressed, very polished, impressively beautiful in the way rich well-put-together women often were. And the other—

Gina gulped.

Laurel Conner had mentioned Doug's realtor. But the one in the parking lot wasn't the woman Gina expected to see.

Instead, turning her head in Gina's direction, stood Amelia Gardner. Parent nemesis. Gina reminded herself of the other time she'd seen Amelia out here, subbing for Doug's realtor.

Could the situation get any messier?

"Oh, thank goodness. Gina. Ms. Prine," said Laurel Conner, catching sight of her too. "Thanks for coming over."

The other two women had swiveled to stare at Gina, hands on hips. Both sets of eyes were hard.

"Ms. Prine, I was just telling these two ladies that Mr. McNally had spent a lot of time picking out the art, and that I just don't. . ." She faltered. Looked over at the other two. Appealed to them. "I hope you can see that," she said to them. "Mr. McNally picked out this art personally. I don't think it's right to throw it out."

"What's she doing here?" drawled Amelia Gardner. "What business is it of yours what my client does with her property?" She directed this rude remark at Gina.

"I'm not sure I—" Gina began.

Amelia turned her attention back to Laurel. "Ms. Conner. This is Mrs. McNally's property. Hers and her husband's. I'm sure you can appreciate that."

"Actually, Mrs. Gardner, we have insurance covenants that say, while the property is under construction, the buyer can of course have access to purchased property. But the whole complex is still under the control of the Currituck Cove Golf Club Association."

"Looks finished to me." That, from Doug's wife.

"Well, of course we see your dilemma, Ms. Conner." Amelia talked over the woman to Laurel, sweet as pie. "You're stuck between a rock and a hard place. The insurance company and the condo owner. That's why I brought Mrs. McNally over here myself, since I have the key and access to the lockbox. But Mrs. McNally isn't disturbing property belonging to the golf club. This is her own property. This art."

With horror, Gina watched Amelia Gardner prod a hoard of paintings and other art objects with her toe.

They were piled up higgledy-piggledy on the asphalt.

"Don't worry, Jaclin," said Amelia to Doug's wife. "We'll sort this out. This is your own property. This is her own property," she told Laurel, a glint in her eye. "Do we have to call the sheriff over this?"

"Oh—" Laurel Conner faltered.

"Look," said Gina, wading into the middle of the mess. "This is very valuable art, and it shouldn't be dumped in the middle of a parking lot. It could be damaged. Some of these pieces are fragile."

"This?" shrilled Jaclin McNally. "You call this art? A kid could have done some of this."

Gina gave her a level look. "I'm sure people can differ on that, Mrs. McNally. Art is a matter of taste." She badly wanted to add, *and yours looks to be atrocious*. She refrained. "The truth is, your husband spent a lot of money on this. How about if I take charge of it. I'll keep it safe, and then you and he can decide what to do with it later on. I'll give you a receipt for it, if you like. I have records of the purchase prices for each piece. If you do hate the art, I can appreciate why you won't want it in your new home. But I'm afraid someone needs to take care of it properly, or you stand to lose a lot of money." There. She'd played the money card. She hoped she was taking the right tone with this woman.

Amelia Gardner rounded on her. "Just what is your interest in all this, Ms. Prine? How is this situation any business of yours?"

Jaclin McNally was looking down sullenly at her feet.

In the sudden spurt of anger that took her over, Gina wasn't sure how she would have answered. What fantastic luck. Theo picked that moment to return her call.

"Theo," she said into the phone, trying to still her ragged breathing.

"Oh. Theo." Jaclin McNally made a disgusted face. Gina turned her back on the woman.

"Theo, I'm glad you called," said Gina. "I'm in the parking lot of the club. Mrs. McNally and the realtor are here, and Mrs. Mc-Nally has taken the art out of Doug's—uh—Mr. McNally's storage room and has dumped it on the pavement." She waited while Theo swore. Then she handed the phone to Jaclin McNally. "Mr. Greene would like to speak to you."

She stepped away. Amelia Gardner glared at her, but Gina ig-nored that. She tried not to eavesdrop on the Jaclin side of the con-versation. Instead, she took Laurel Conner aside. "Thanks for get-ting in touch with me, Laurel," she said. The club director looked to be practically in tears. "It was the only thing to do, under the cir-cumstances. Mrs. McNally and Mrs. Gardner are right, though. I shouldn't be involved. But I can see you had no choice. Now let's let Mr. McNally's financial advisor handle this. I'll wait in the car. If you need me to take the art with me, I'll be glad to do it."

"Also, they have your phone," said Laurel grimly.

"Also that."

Privately, she wished Laurel had just discreetly packed up the art and stored it somewhere safe until Doug got back. But Laurel didn't want to step into the middle of some husband-wife brouha-ha any more than Gina did.

Well, now Theo would make it all okay. Gina had confidence he would.

And he did. At least to the extent he convinced Jaclin McNally that no matter what she personally thought about it, the art was valuable, and if she didn't want to lose a lot of money, she'd make sure it was safe.

"Okay," said Jaclin, handing the phone back to Gina. She turned to Laurel. "Guess this stuff has to stay. Don't give it to that woman, though." She looked over at Gina the way she might look at a slug crawling across the pavement. Her head swiveled back to Laurel. "Guess just stick all this stuff back in that storage room." She shrugged and turned away. "That gay prick," Gina heard her mutter.

"Will you see to the re-packing, Ms. Conner?" said Amelia sweetly.

"Yes, I'll get some of the employees to put the art back where it came from," said Laurel, her voice completely colorless.

"Good," said Amelia. She gave Gina a malicious smile. "Getting into the art consulting business now, are we?" She turned to Laurel. "I'm not sure why being some local art teacher makes Ms. Prine an expert, but whatever."

Gina made no reply.

Jaclin was already halfway across the parking lot to her car by then. Amelia caught up with her, and the two walked away togeth-er.

Gina and Laurel stood watching them go.

"I apologize for dragging you into this, Ms. Prine," said Laurel after a moment. "I don't understand Mrs. Gardner at all. I have to tell you, when I saw her with Mrs. McNally, and not the regular realtor, I wanted to hide."

"I think I know what you mean," said Gina with a grim smile.

"I don't understand it, though. Mrs. Gardner told me you're the one I should call about the art, that everyone knew you were the one advising Mr. McNally about the art, and then, when you got here, she treated you so rudely."

"Don't worry about it," Gina said, although she felt a pang of alarm. Oh well. Amelia Gardner was just a shit-disturber, a shit-disturber to the bone, and once she saw a way to stir up a little shit, it was irresistible to her. Catnip to a cat. That's all that was. But she said only, "Theo is the one who needed to get involved, and in the end, we got in touch with him. Now it's their problem. Mr. and Mrs. McNally's. But those two women just made a lot of work for you, and I'm sorry they did."

Laurel smiled at her gratefully. Past her, Gina could see some of the hotel employees carefully settling the art on dollies.

"Put this ridiculous incident out of your mind, Laurel. I know I'll put it out of mine," she said as she got back in her car to drive home.

Once there, she felt a weariness so deep she wanted to cry. She fell into bed without bothering about supper. Just before she did, she gave herself a long look in the bathroom mirror.

That was a lie, she told herself, thinking of how she had tried to reassure Laurel Conner. I won't be able to put this out of my mind. It's going to eat me alive. Especially that last part about Amelia Gardner. Amelia Gardner actually urging Laurel to call her and then, when she got there, casting Gina as some intruding villain. Just more Amelia Gardner drama, she guessed.

She stared at herself. Disheveled, exhausted, bags under her eyes from the late night with Archer. She thought about the pristine Jaclin McNally. A lovely ornament for a man like Doug to cherish. Some aging frat-boy. Some aging jock.

So, she told herself. Mrs. McNally is very much in the picture. And that's enough of Doug.

If only that traitor, her body, would believe it.

Bombshell

THE LAST DAY OF THE last tournament, on a beautiful links course in Devon, the sun lying low in the west, Doug finished over par. It had been a good day nonetheless. He'd hit some really good shots, only to have those gains eaten away by some really bad ones, especially as he tired on the back nine.

It's beautiful here. But I'll be glad to get home, he thought. He was a bit uneasy, though. Theo had emailed something about a problem. Some vague thing about saving it for when Doug was back in the States, no use fretting about it long-distance. What could Theo mean? Maybe his finances weren't in as good shape as he thought.

He smiled to himself as he strolled toward the clubhouse, though. Home. Home didn't mean Charlotte, and drama, and scenes. It meant peace. Currituck Cove. It meant, well, okay, he was going to say it to himself. It meant Gina.

He had decided something. He decided he was going to try, with Gina. At least see where it goes, he said to himself. The divorce decree should be coming in soon. Then he'd really give it a try. What was there to lose? All she could say was no. All she could do was reject him. Maybe, if they really did give it a go, they'd see they were wrong for each other, and if they did, he'd behave like an adult and step away. But suppose instead. . .

His heart thumped in his chest. He felt a familiar tightening of his dick against his pants leg. Down, boy.

Well, he'd think the whole thing through on the plane. Tomorrow he'd head to London, spend the night in a hotel, get himself to Heathrow in the morning, and then home. Fly into JFK, transfer to a plane taking him to Raleigh-Durham. The plan was, Theo would pick him up at RDU, they'd both go over to visit Doug's dad at the nursing home to get some financial matters settled there. Doug's dad needed to sign a power of attorney, for one thing. And, yes, try to talk to the old coot like a reasonable adult, even though every time Doug tried, his dad treated him as if he were thirteen, and still pulling kid stuff like smoking weed behind the middle school or getting into the bourbon. After that thankless duty, Theo would drive Doug down the coast. And Doug would prepare to step into a brand-new life.

He whisked into the golf course locker room, determined to stop thinking about any of it. London tomorrow, then home. He made himself think instead about the game he'd just played, the highs and lows. But especially the beautiful landscape, the quality of the light. He laughed a little, too. Maybe his brief moment of fame some months earlier had produced a fan or two. Normally, a crowd of fans accompanied the men on the leader board from hole to hole as they played. Those at the back of the pack, almost never, unless a few family members or friends had come out.

Strange. Doug had noticed one man doggedly following him every step as he played. A young man, looked to be in his thirties. What was stranger, he had in tow a little boy, just a toddler. Three years old, something like that. Old enough to traipse around with his daddy. Young enough to need to be hoisted up on his daddy's shoulders when he got fretful or tired. A few times Doug had to

make an effort to put this fan of his out of mind. He needed to concentrate on his game. But always, out of the corner of his eye, there
the man stood.

Was this guy responsible for that double bogey, he wondered,
re-playing it in his mind as he showered. Nah. That was completely
on him. Once, the little boy had actually waved at him. Not exactly
golf etiquette, but Doug grinned and waved back. His next shot
off the tee went better. Maybe the little boy was his lucky charm.
When he came out, he was so absorbed in his thoughts that he
didn't notice the man and small child, the same two, standing in
the clubhouse lobby.

"Sir."

Doug looked up. So, yeah. A fan. Doug looked for the pen to
come whipping out of a pocket. A program to sign. "Yes?"

"Douglas McNally."

"Yes."

"My name is John Richards. This is Ruan."

Doug bent over and smiled at the little boy. "Hello, Ruan. I saw
you out there." He stood up. He and John Richards were around
the same height. The man was tall, sandy-haired. "Think Ruan will
be a golfer when he grows up? What can I do for you, John?"

"I believe—" John Richards took a deep breath.

Doug stared at him, puzzled.

John Richards dropped his bombshell. "I believe you're my father, sir. And Ruan is your grandson."

"What?" Doug felt a catch in his chest, the feeling of an almost
physical blow. What could this man be telling him. "You were out
there." He didn't know what to say. "You followed me."

"Yes, I did. I thought about finding a phone number, maybe
calling first. . ." John Richards trailed off. "I thought at first Ruan

and I would just take a look, and then we'd go home. But at the end of the day, I just thought. . ."

"Richards." What a dolt, Doug said to himself. Richards. Of course. "You're Tressa's son." Tressa Richards. She must have taken her own name back when she left him. Who would blame her?

"That's right."

"But your mother and I, we didn't—" They hadn't had children.

John Richards smiled. He wrote something down on a piece of paper he fished from his pocket, and handed it to Doug. "That's my birthday."

Doug did a quick mental calculation. The time matched up. He recalled the day Tressa left him, the day he'd found her note. He recalled wondering if he should rush to the airport and try to stop her, like some rom-com movie ending. He recalled the moment he realized her flight had already taken off. And this man. This man standing in front of him with his little son. This man had been born about seven months later. Doug was floored. When Tressa left him, she had been pregnant. And she'd never told him. He'd never even suspected. Less than nine months after she'd left him, John Richards came into the world.

"I don't know what to say." Doug stared intently at the younger man. His son.

"Sorry to tell you like this. I see it's a mistake. I'm in the wrong, and I do apologize. I didn't plan to tell you at all. Just. . .catch a glimpse of you. When the time came for me and Ruan to go home, I waited for you instead," John said simply. "I don't understand it myself. Why open old wounds?"

"But I'm glad you have," said Doug. "I didn't even know you existed. I'm glad I know." His eyes moved to Ruan. "I'm glad to set eyes on this young man." A powerful feeling was struggling to get out of Doug, and he recognized it now. Joy. A completely unexpected surge of joy.

Ruan snuggled under his father's arm and stuck a thumb in his mouth.

"I'm leaving for the States in the morning," said Doug. "That's much too soon. I have so many questions."

"I've followed your career all my life," said John. "When I realized you were here, and so close, I had to see you. I had to come face to face with you."

"So you've always known you were my son. And I've never known I even had a son. I don't have any children. Didn't think I did." Doug laughed a little. "But this is marvelous. And a grandchild!"

"My mother never kept it from me."

"What you must have thought of me. A man who never made the least effort to know his own child."

"Mother never said much about it. She just said things hadn't worked out between the two of you, and that you were far away. She never led me to think she hated you. Nothing like that. It was just a fact of life. I didn't think about it much. But later on, I did. I wondered. At the end of her life, she—" John stopped, clearly moved.

"I was very sorry to hear that Tressa died. She was a lovely woman. I only found out about it through a mutual acquaintance, and months later. I didn't even know how to get in touch. Didn't know if she had remarried, had family. Anything."

John looked at Doug. "She told me before she died. That you didn't know about me. That she'd kept it from you. She told me she was sorry, but that it was too late, and I should let it go. It always worried her, that I watched all your tournaments on the telly. She worried I'd want to know you, and that you'd reject me. I think that's what went through her mind."

"How sad," said Doug. "Sad that Tressa would think that. And very sad for me."

"Don't hate her," John said, low. "She was trying to protect me, I think."

"Of course I don't hate her. I never did, and I don't now."

After a while, John said he had to get Ruan back to his mum. They shook hands. Impulsively, Doug drew John to him and hugged him, not exactly the English thing to do. John stepped back, stiff and clearly uncomfortable. But Ruan allowed himself to be hugged, and giggled when Doug tickled him.

John and Doug agreed they'd talk further on the phone, once Doug was home. And Doug promised he'd be back for a visit, or bring John and his family to the States to visit, if they liked. He certainly didn't want to push. But his heart was bursting. A son! A grandson! Doug wasn't sure what John himself really wanted. The Brits. Inscrutable to us Yanks, he thought. Still, John was the one who had initiated the contact. So he must want it.

When Doug got on the plane to fly westward, his mind was full of this new strange development in his life, and not at all on Gina. That had been his plan, to spend the hours of plane travel thinking about her, and what he should do about his feelings for her. Does life ever work out the way we expect it to? he asked himself.

No. No, it doesn't.

What the heart wants

THEY WERE TUCKED INTO their favorite booth at The Mermaid. Gina looked across affectionately at the other two. My posse, she thought. My crew. She grinned at herself, but she felt kind of stupid, too.

Why is it I'm the one always so needy, she thought. Fran knew herself, exactly who she was and what she wanted. So did Bunny. Why was it Gina turned out to be the one up in the air all the time? The flake of the threesome. No matter how hard she tried to turn herself against Doug, there she was, moments later, thinking about Doug. Just as a for instance.

The other two were not fooled, at least not about her state of mind.

"Something's going on," said Fran. "We can tell."

"We know you're beating yourself up over something. Spill it, girlfriend." Bunny.

"Just in one of my usual messes. What an airhead."

"You're anything but an airhead, Gina," said Fran.

"Oh, let's not talk about the mess I make of my life. Lots of good things are going on," said Gina. "Did I tell you how well I did this year at the Southport crafts fair?"

She spent many minutes filling her friends in on her Southport experience. "And Archer wants me to exhibit in his Wilmington gallery now. And, get this, in his Charlotte gallery."

As Fran and Bunny were woohooing over that, Gina sat back, sipping her iced tea. There. That should divert them.

Sweet tea, the national drink of the South. Even after all this time, Gina had to remind Paula that she liked hers without all the sugar.

"A sure sign of a Yankee," said Fran, grinning. "Load mine up with extra, Paula."

"But I don't want any sugar either, Paula," said Bunny. No one, listening to Bunny's sweet-as-sugar drawl, would ever mistake Bunny for some Yankee. But Bunny cheated. She stirred artificial sweetener into hers.

"Archer sounds like a wonderful guy," said Fran carefully, taking a big swig of her sugary drink. "Giving you roses. Making you dinner."

"Uh. Well. Archer asked me to marry him."

The other two leaned forward breathlessly. "And?" said Fran.

"I. Uh. I said no."

They slumped back into their side of the booth.

"Why no? He sounds lovely," said Fran after a moment.

"He IS lovely. I just don't love him."

"So," said Fran. "Love. That's the main thing, huh."

Gina and Bunny looked at each other. They knew Fran had a long-running off-again on-again relationship with a lawyer in Elizabeth City. They had both wondered what Fran was going to do about it.

"I've told Nelson I'll marry him," she said, conversationally.

More woohooing.

Paula the waitress came over to refill their glasses. "You ladies are clearly celebrating. Need something a little stronger?"

"Thanks, Paula, but I'm on my lunch break. Can't go back to the bank with liquor on my breath, much as I'd like to." Fran leaned forward intently after Paula left. "See, I'm not sure what I feel for Nelson is love. Not exactly. I do love him. Just not in that swoony way most people mean when they say the word love. But I respect him, our friendship is solid. We share values. We have a lot in common."

"I think that's great, Fran," said Gina. "You've known Nelson forever. You know the type of man he is."

Fran smiled. "Kind. Smart. Yeah. His daughter and I really like each other, too, and you know? In these later-in-life marriages, that means a lot." Fran had been widowed very young. Her husband, in the military, hadn't come back from Kuwait. Gina was glad Fran had grabbed some happiness for herself.

As for Bunny. She was an ardent subscriber to the Man-of-the-Month Club. She found them on dating apps. Then she discarded them. "What do I need with a man complicating my life? Men are good for one thing." She winked.

The friends spent most of the rest of their lunch getting filled in on Fran's wedding plans.

But at the end, when they were getting ready to go about their day, Bunny slammed her hands down on the table. "Hold it right there. I still want to know what's going on with you, Gina. And you still haven't told us."

"Yes, she has," said Fran. "She told us she turned Archer down. Is it a done deal?" she said to Gina. "Can you tell him yes? I think you should tell him yes."

"Hey, is all this gallery stuff just so you'll say yes?" Bunny's eyes narrowed suspiciously. "What about now you've rejected him. Will he still want your stuff in his gallery?"

"Oh," said Gina. "Goodness. Archer made it clear before I left that whatever I decide, he wants my things in his gallery."

"Sounds like a stand-up kind of guy," said Fran. "I like him more and more."

"As for the marriage question. We left it open," said Gina, feeling miserable. "We left it like, I'll think about it."

"Say yes," said Fran.

"Say no," said Bunny.

"Bunny!" Fran shook her head at Bunny.

"No, but look at her," Bunny told Fran, tilting her head toward Gina. "We know the real problem. Don't we. Gina doesn't love Archer. She does love—"

"Shh," said Gina, looking around hastily. "Let's not talk about it. No telling who will overhear in this gossipy place. And Bunny, we both know whatever I might feel about it, that thing—that other thing—can't happen. It was wrong to begin with. And now. Now it's got complications."

"I'll say it has," said Bunny, with relish.

Gina stared at Bunny, horrified.

"A town this small, you can't keep anything private, certainly not a juicy piece of drama like that, Gina." She took care to lower her voice. "You and Jaclin McNally, facing off in the parking lot of the golf club. And who has the biggest mouth in all Currituck Cove? Who's the town's biggest loudmouth?"

"Amelia Gardner," said Fran, starting to look horrified too.

They all slid out of the booth. Fran needed to get back to the bank. Gina needed to get to her workroom, and Bunny was putting the finishing touches on the little showroom she was starting to call her atelier.

"For what it's worth," said Fran at the door of The Mermaid, looking back at Gina. "I'm on Team Archer."

"I'm on Team Doug," said Bunny.

The other two turned on her, furiously shushing her. Unconcerned, she waved goodbye and strolled to the hotpinkmobile, flicking her blonde lob over one shoulder.

For the rest of the day, Gina tried hard to settle her mind on her work. It had tripled. Not only did she have to get ready for the mountain crafts fairs coming right up, but now she also owed Archer some of her best pieces. She had some great ideas for the designs. The absorbing work hardly felt like work at all, until she stopped to think about the pressure.

She took a mid-afternoon break, though. Father Laughton was due to come over to pick out something for his wife Nancy's birthday.

"How's everything at St. Hilda's, Father?" said Gina, opening her front door and ushering him in. "I thought we'd have coffee out in my sun room, and I'll show you some things I think Nancy will really love. If you don't see anything you like, I have a lot more in the workroom."

"Thank you, Gina. St. Hilda's is fine, except we're missing our alto."

"I'm back for a few weeks before my next craft fair starts, so I'll be there Sunday," she said.

She settled him in the sun room and brought out a tray of pins and pendants for him to look over.

"Nancy will go for this one," said Father Laughton, picking out a pewter pin in a Celtic knot design. He and Gina concluded their business swiftly, and then Gina persuaded him to stay for another cup of coffee and a cookie from the little bake shop down the beach, everyone's favorite.

"Gina," said Father Laughton, looking at her carefully over the rim of his mug. "You don't have to answer this, but is anything wrong?"

Gina guessed everything had been bottled up inside her so long it all came spilling out now.

"So," she concluded tearfully, "I'm a terrible Christian, I've led a life full of mistakes, and now I might be on the verge of another big one, just when I thought I'd gotten it all together."

"First of all," said Father Laughton, "You are not a terrible Christian. Every one of us makes mistakes, and lord knows the Lord knows that. And loves us anyway. This big mistake you say you're on the verge of. What's going on there?"

"Ugh, you've probably heard this one a thousand times over the course of your career, Father. I'm in love with a man I shouldn't be in love with. I think it's love, anyway." Gina sighed. "Everyone in town knows about that incident in the golf club parking lot, don't they?"

"It's a small town, Gina," said Father Laughton, shrugging and smiling.

"This spring and into the summer, I was advising a new resident, Mr. McNally, on his art purchases. His financial advisor Mr. Greene accompanied us on all the trips around the region we took to look at art. No funny business took place."

"The only people—person—implying any funny business took place knows very well none did. She's just a—"

Shit-disturber, Gina supplied mentally.

"—trouble-maker," Father Laughton concluded smoothly. "And everyone in town knows she is. So that's all on her, not on you. People like that make their own trouble, and it almost always comes back on themselves. I feel sorry for people like that."

Yeah, but you're not her target, thought Gina sourly. Then, in an almost physically palpable way, the memory of that kiss swooped down on her. The kiss Doug had planted on her, right on her own front porch, and how much it had thrilled her. The feeling of his body, his maleness pressed against her, and how much she wanted it.

"But Father," said Gina in a small voice. "He's married. Even though he said he was getting a divorce. And then suddenly there's his wife in the golf club parking lot. And I—" She hesitated. "I know it's wrong. I have feelings for him. And I think he has feelings for me. See there? I'm a terrible person."

"Someone once said—" Father Laughlin took her hands in his. "Someone once wrote, 'The heart wants what the heart wants.' That's just human nature, Gina. The feelings aren't wrong. It's what we do about them."

When Father Laughton left, Gina still didn't know what to do about her feelings. But she had told someone who understood. She felt a sense of relief. For about a minute.

The next day, she opened her door to find a little brown-paper-wrapped package on her doorstep, tied with string. Gina opened the package. Mystified, she lifted out a book. *The Letters of Emily Dickinson*. Then she noticed a bookmark. She opened the book to the page it marked and read the underlined words.

The heart wants what the heart wants. . . .

See you in court

DOUG SAT RIGIDLY IN the office of his expensive Charlotte lawyer, Howard. Across the polished rosewood table from Doug and Howard, Jaclin refused to make eye contact. She sat beside her own lawyer, a woman known as a real shark of a divorce attorney. The "I'll take you to the cleaners" kind.

Look at me, Jaclin. He sent a silent message across the gap.

It must have worked. "I don't want this, Doug," said Jaclin in her sweetest tones. She had deliberately dressed like a darling innocent, all white pique, her hair in sunny highlights, her tan, her provocative little mouth. "We're equally at fault. Can't we put it behind us? Begin us again?"

"Equally at fault!" Doug spluttered, but Howard held up a hand in caution. Doug sank back into Howard's opulent leather conference room chair.

"Sarah," Howard said, addressing Jaclin's attorney. "I don't think this meeting is at all wise. Since you've insisted, though, I hope you realize that Mr. McNally has video footage of Mrs. McNally in a compromising position with another man."

"Oh, Howard." The woman smiled disarmingly. "You know how grainy those videos are. They could be anyone. My client is prepared to argue they are not videos of her at all. As for the man in question, you can't even see his face, not enough to identify him. Who's to say those videos are not a fake."

"They're not a fake," growled Doug. Howard raised a hand to silence him again.

The rest of the meeting passed in unpleasant jockeying between the two attorneys.

At the end, Howard cleared his throat. "I should bring up another thing. Mrs. McNally was caught lying to Mr. McNally's realtor in an attempt to enter Mr. McNally's domicile and take or damage some of his belongings."

"You know as well as I, Howard," Jaclin's lawyer countered. "That golf villa is marital property. Mrs. McNally had every right to be there."

"We will argue it's not marital property at all. Mr. McNally paid cash for the condo from a bequest to him by his mother. That's all documented, Sarah."

"A very debatable position, Howard," said Jaclin's attorney smoothly.

Doug glanced aside at Howard, for Howard's I-told-you-so-but-would-you-listen glance back. Howard was too much of a professional to do it.

"In addition," said Jaclin's attorney—and Doug was infuriated to see a tiny smirk begin to curl Jaclin's lips—"It was clear to Mrs. McNally that another woman was involved in the attempt to keep Mrs. McNally from rightfully disposing of her own property. Who was that woman, Mr. McNally? What is your relationship to her?" Jaclin's lawyer addressed this directly to Doug.

God, Doug thought. She means Gina. I've dragged Gina into this shitstorm somehow.

"Don't answer that, Doug," said Howard. He nodded to the two across the table. "Sarah. Mrs. McNally. See you in court."

Doug looked over his shoulder at Jaclin, as she and her lawyer headed for the door. "Give my best to Pompom," he said.

After they were gone, Howard sat looking at Doug. "So? Some other woman involved here, Doug?"

"No!" Doug exclaimed. He got to his feet and opened the conference room door. "Theo, could you please come in here?"

Theo had been waiting just outside. He came in, shaking his head. "Jaclin gave me a dirty look as she went past. She doesn't like me much. Ready to talk over your daddy issues, Doug?"

"That too, but tell Howard about Gina. Jaclin was just implying dirty stuff about her."

Theo filled Howard in about the incident in the parking lot. "Gina Prine has behaved impeccably," he concluded, "And she behaved impeccably in that parking lot, too, after a lot of provocation.

"What's this about daddy issues?" Howard said after he'd taken notes about Gina Prine and agreed with Doug and Theo that Gina was a problem Jaclin had manufactured.

"Now for Dad," said Doug grimly. "This involves Theo, too." Doug told Howard about his father's latest curmudgeonly refusal to sign a power of attorney. The more his dementia worsened, the more dug in he became.

Theo sighed. He began opening his briefcase. He looked up at Howard. "Doug isn't getting a penny from his father's estate. Well, a little bit. Not much. I suppose you know all about it, and so do I, as Doug's money manager. I tried to talk to Mr. McNally, too, but he just accused me of being in cahoots with his son to take his money, and then he screamed insults at me." Specifically, anti-gay slurs. Theo tried to will the memory away.

"Damn," muttered Doug. "Dad has always been an asshole, but now, with the dementia, the filter's come off."

Howard shook his head. "These situations are so tough."

"But anyway," Theo went on. "Mr. McNally has tied his entire estate up in a trust that goes to his favorite cause, an endowment he is making to a big tennis complex that will have his name on it. Doug and his brother are getting a pittance. But Doug has to get power of attorney from the old boy in order to make decisions about the nursing home, pay his dad's bills, and so forth. And now his dad has started squawking about how Doug is trying to take advantage of him. How Doug has stuck him in the nursing home as a way to get his hands on the old guy's fortune."

As they left, Doug felt a hopelessness descend on him. They had returned to the Jaclin problem at the end of their session. "That video really does show Jaclin," he told Howard, standing in the doorway to the conference room.

"I know it does," said Howard with a sigh. "Jaclin has hired herself a very smart lawyer, though. Sarah knows how to get that kind of thing thrown out in court."

"I should post it on social media," Doug growled.

"No!" exclaimed Theo.

"No, don't," said Howard. "Revenge porn. Not a good idea. It's a felony in North Carolina. Talk about giving Sarah enough rope to hang you." He ran a hand across his forehead.

"Hang him out to dry, anyway," said Theo.

"Howard." Doug frowned. "I don't understand any of this. Jaclin was all for the divorce only a month or two ago. Now this."

"Money, Doug. It's all about money. She's going to try to make you pay. She sees dollar signs, the big tournament win you had, the condo she thinks she can grab. Money, and sticking it to you."

"Sounds about right," said Doug morosely. He turned to Theo. "Howard's a class act. He's not telling me I Told You So over buying the house on the golf course before the divorce was final."

"I'm not either, bro. Water under the bridge. Let Howard handle it. You're more than a match for Sarah," Theo turned to say to Howard.

"I do my best," said Howard, ushering them out.

"Ugh," said Doug as he and Theo drove out of Charlotte. "First my dad. Then Jaclin. What did I do in a former life to deserve those two?"

"Must've been something really bad," said Theo, taking the exit onto I-85.

Doug settled back. They planned to trade off driving, stop for lunch. Then, late in the afternoon, they'd reach the coast. They'd reach Currituck Cove where, the nice club director assured him, his golf villa was ready for occupancy.

And he hoped it stayed his.

He felt a little thrill of excitement. Getting back to the beach life. Seeing Gina!

Even so, he couldn't lift his gloom. He kept obsessing about Jaclin. About his dad. "What did I do to deserve them," he said. "And what did they do to deserve me. Is it a case of we deserve each other, Theo?"

Theo glanced aside at his friend, then back to the road. "Nah, bud. Nothing anyone could do would ever deserve your dad. Hitler, maybe. As for Jaclin—"

"Ego," said Doug. "If not for that, I would never have married that bitch. A big swelled head, plus not being able to keep Mr. Dougie in my pants, where he belonged."

"And I love you anyway," said Theo lightly.

"But I notice you're not exactly disagreeing with that last statement of mine, Theo, old buddy."

Theo just laughed.

They drove all the way across North Carolina on I-40. At last they stopped for a late lunch in Williamston, where they'd fork off onto Highway 17.

"I hate to stop so close to home," said Doug. Already he was thinking of Currituck Cove as home. "I can practically smell the ocean from here. But we need to eat, and I think I'll be too tired for anything more complicated than fast food takeout once we get there. Besides, I haven't told you something, Theo. Something important."

"Uh oh," said Theo. "I tell ya, buddy. I've had about as much as I can handle."

"No, this is a good thing," said Doug.

They pulled off in Williamston into the parking lot of a quaint little diner, and went in, ordering plates of okra and grits and fried chicken to give themselves the energy for the final push to Currituck Cove.

Once they were settled at a window of the diner, Doug said, "Here's something I guess I should have shared with Howard, while we were in his office. I'm still processing it, though."

"What?" said Theo.

"Theo. I have a son."

"You have a what?" Theo whistled. "Talk about daddy issues. Good god, Doug, you needed to tell Howard about this."

"It has nothing to do with Jaclin. Ghost of a past life. When Tressa left me, she was pregnant."

"And she never told you."

"No, never did. But before she died, she told her son. Our son. I mean, all those years, he's known about me, Theo. But he never knew I didn't want him. That I hadn't deliberately kept away from him. That's what Tressa told him, there at the end. That I had no idea he existed. That it wasn't my fault I'd never reached out to him."

"Wow. You found this out in England?"

"Yep." Doug filled Theo in on how he'd learned about John. "Even better, Theo—" Doug leaned forward eagerly. "I have a son AND a grandson."

"Aww, Doug. Wow. Just wow. What are their names?"

"Tressa took her family name back when she left me."

"Richards," said Theo, remembering.

"Yeah. My son's name is John Richards. And my grandson is Ruan. He's three. I haven't met my daughter-in-law yet. I want to bring them all to the States for a visit. I'll wait til this mess with Jaclin is over, though."

"Man," said Theo. "That's wonderful, Doug." His eyes were soft. Then they hardened. "Your son. He found this out through his mother?"

"Yeah. We talked about it. He said he'd never bothered with one of those DNA tests. He said he didn't want anything from me, didn't care whether I believed him or not. Just wanted to meet me." Doug looked down. He saw his hands were trembling. "He said he wanted Ruan to meet me." He gave Theo a long look. "You think this is some scam? But what would he have to gain from it? Especially since he said he didn't want anything from me. I mean, I do okay, and that's thanks to you, bud. But I'm not filthy rich or anything. I'm not gonna get anything much from my dad." His jaw tightened. "I don't want anything from him, either."

"But does John Richards know that? I'm just a naturally suspicious character, I guess," said Theo with a sigh. "Yeah, what does he have to gain? And anyway, how would he even know about your dad. Anyone who has a brain knows, great, you won some prize money at a big tournament, but that's not gonna last."

Doug shook his head. "Why doesn't Jaclin see that. Why isn't her lawyer telling her that?"

"My guess, her lawyer is saying grab it while you can."

"Yeah. Probably. But then there's this new thing. My son. So when I start to feel down or get mad enough to commit murder—revenge porn, anyway—" He gave Theo a rueful grin. "Then I think about finding out I have a son. And a grandson. I think about the really important stuff."

"Hey," said Theo, smiling at Doug. "It sounds great, bro. Do you have pictures."

"Yes, look," said Doug, beaming, opening his phone, scrolling to the photos, handing the phone to Theo.

Theo took a look. He shook his head. "Doug. Count me in. I'm a believer. John Richards is the spitting image of you when you were a young buck."

"He is? I sort of don't know."

"He definitely is. I can see Tressa in him, too."

"You always liked Tressa."

"Yeah," said Theo.

"You thought I didn't treat Tressa right. And you're on the money there, bro. I didn't."

"Nothing to do about it now," said Theo gently. "If only we could take back all our youthful mistakes."

In his excitement, Doug was already past it. "And look at this!" He thrust the phone at Theo again. "That's an old photo. I digitized a bunch of the family snapshots when Mom died. That's me, that's my mom. That's my dad. The baby is Stan." Stan, Doug's younger brother.

"Huh," said Theo. "Your dad was actually pretty good looking, as a young guy."

"Yeah. Anyway, there's the three-year-old me. Now take a look at this."

Theo did a double-take. "That's Ruan?"

"Yeah."

"A little Dougie if there ever was one."

"I think so."

"Man, look at you, from no family to an entire crew of them." Theo waved a hand dismissively. "Your dad and Stan don't count."

"Don't be too hard on Stan."

"He just dumped the whole dad problem on you, bro."

"I know." Doug sighed. "Stan goes his own way. Always has. He wants no part of it. I don't blame Stan. I blame my dad for driving him away, and my mom for letting my dad get away with it."

Theo didn't say anything to that, just drank his coffee. "Okay, bro. Ready for the last leg of the trip?"

They got back on the road. And when Doug sniffed that first sea breeze, that first saltiness in the air, he felt a peace descend on him.

It didn't last long. The closer they got to Currituck Cove, the more Doug thought about Gina. The more he thought about Gina, the more excited—in every way—he found himself getting.

"Doug," Theo began.

It was as if Doug could read Theo's mind. Yeah, he told himself. Theo's right. Reluctantly, he said it out loud. "I know what you're thinking, Theo, and you're right. I guess. . . Jaclin being Jaclin, and already somehow getting Gina mixed up with the problems between us, I better not see Gina."

"I think that's wise," said Theo. "Jaclin and that crazy realtor, I dunno. They somehow sniffed out something between you and Gina."

"There's nothing between me and Gina," said Doug, defensively.

"Uh huh," said Theo.

It was a dark and steamy night

FRAN AND GINA DROVE Bunny to the Norfolk airport. She was headed to Scottsdale where, to Fran's astonishment, there really was a strong Adorable Me presence.

"Selling Adorée and Mélisande, of course," said Bunny. "And I'm invited to their big sales conference, to learn the best marketing methods. My atelier is almost ready. People are moving into those condos and golf villas. When I get back next week, I'll be rarin' to go."

Fran and Gina hugged Bunny at Departures and watched as she strutted with her roll-on through the doors of the airport.

"There she goes. Watch out, world. Watch out, Scottsdale."

"Yeah, but Paris?" said Fran.

"Fran, who cares if there's an Adorable Me rep in Paris. In Bunny's fantasy world, there is. That's all the counts."

"Yeah," said Fran, looking affectionately after Bunny. "There's only one Bunny."

Gina and Fran grinned at each other, and Fran, who was driving, took them home. She didn't drop Gina off at her house, though. She dropped Gina off at Bunny's house right on the beach.

While Bunny was in Scottsdale, Gina had taken on the task of house-sitter. She was between craft fairs, and staying in Bunny's house was something nice she could do for her friend. Best of all, there was a lot in it for Gina. She was not only house-sitting. She was dog-sitting. Bingo-sitting. What could be better? As dog-deprived as she felt, it was a positive luxury to spend the week at Bunny's.

Besides, she knew she could use a little time on the beach. Walking the sand, kicking through the surf. That always eased her. Not that she couldn't drive over to the public access and do it any time. But being at Bunny's made it easier.

Damn it. Her unease was all about Doug. Knowing he was back. Knowing they were in the same town and couldn't, shouldn't see each other.

He may not even want to, she told herself. All these feelings I have? They may be all mine, and anything I imagined on his part is just that, imagination.

Of course, that kiss...

Whenever she thought about it, her breath kind of stopped.

Who knew, though. He might be the kind of man who did things like that and didn't think a thing about them. She didn't even know him. Not really.

All of their days looking at art gave that misgiving the lie. She felt she'd come to know him.

Then that awful incident with his wife. Just thinking about it made Gina blush. Somehow, his wife must see her as some kind of threat. Otherwise, why create that kind of scene?

And I'm not, she told herself. Not a threat. Never done anything to make anyone think that.

The kiss. That was between herself and Doug. And she had buried it deep inside herself. It needed to stay buried.

When Fran dropped her off, Gina rushed into Bunny's house to feed Bingo. Being with Bingo took her mind off things like Doug McNally. Pooper-scooper in hand, she set out to give Bingo a quick spin around the block. Later she planned a nice long walk up the beach with him.

Before she could do it, though, she got a phone call from Archer and spent most of the remaining daylight hashing out plans for a new jewelry line.

"You still haven't given me an answer, Gina," he said before he ended the call.

"Answer?" she said, stalling.

"You know what I mean." Archer's voice was silky. "I'm not rushing you. I respect you too much to rush you. Just. . .think about it, okay?"

"Okay," she promised.

"Because I think about you all the time, Gina."

She put her phone down, feeling troubled. Archer was kind, he was a good-looking older man, fit, funny and talented. He wanted to do things for her, pamper her. His interests and hers were compatible. She was sure she'd have a nice life, with Archer. So why wasn't she enthusiastically on Team Archer?

It was twilight by the time she got Bingo's leash out again. But that was okay. The beach was safe, and Bingo was a big dog. Nobody would mess with her while she was with Bingo.

Bingo was panting and smiling in the way only a lab knows how to smile. That is, by wriggling his entire body with joy.

"Ready, boy? Ready for your walk?"

"Yes!" said Bingo, in Dog. "Yes! Yes!"

It was the end of summer. The days were starting to get shorter. By the time Gina and Bingo got very far down the beach, the night was drawing on, full dark. Usually the sea breeze kept everything relatively cool. Tonight was unusually humid. Positively steamy.

Storm coming in, Gina thought, looking out to sea, where the underside of some swollen greenish clouds were taking up the last bit of light.

Once the storm broke, and blew itself out, she knew the moisture would wash out of the air, leaving everything feeling delicious.

As they turned for home, Gina let Bingo off the leash, and he frolicked into the surf, barking and leaping.

The sticky air had plastered Gina's loose shirt tight to her body. The sand felt so good beneath her feet that she kicked off her sandals and walked along the very edge of the water, where the sand was firm and little wavelets kept sweeping in deliciously over her toes.

A big moon, eerie in the strange glistening light of the coming storm, was beginning to rise over the waves.

There was a faint, far-off boom of thunder.

"Bingo!" Gina called. Time to get herself and Bingo back to Bunny's.

Bingo, good dog, came when she called. He let himself be put back on the leash.

With a big sigh, the rain came slanting, shearing in.

"Let's get home, big boy," Gina said to Bingo. They began to run for Bunny's.

But as they made for Bunny's front porch with its protective overhang, Gina suddenly pulled back on Bingo's leash.

A dark shape, a man, huddled on the top step of the porch against one of the pillars.

The figure didn't move.

Bingo yanked his leash from Gina's hand and leaped for the porch stairs. Before Gina could even yell, he was back, leaping around her frantically, darting toward the figure, darting back to Gina.

Gina stared hard. Then she dashed up the steps, bent over the figure. "Doug! Doug!" she cried.

He was unresponsive. He fell over across the plankings of the porch with a thud.

In near-panic, she found Bunny's keys, threw the front door wide. As Bingo bounded anxiously around them, she grabbed Doug by the shirt and dragged him across the threshold and into the house, slamming and locking the door behind them. Gusts of rain had followed them in. She was soaked, Bingo was shaking water all over Bunny's nicely decorated front hall, and Doug was sodden. Sodden and out of it.

"Sodden, all right," thought Gina, leaning over and sniffing the fumes of alcohol misting off him. "Douglas McNally, you are dead drunk," she hissed at him. "And here I worried you were just dead."

Doug stirred. Through the hair flopping into his face, he fixed a bleary eye on her. "Gina. Hi, beautiful," he slurred. He lunged at her, tried to kiss her.

"Hey. None of that. You need to get dry, and dried out, and into bed," she told him.

The dried-out part, she realized, was going to take a while. But dry and into bed? She wondered how she would manage it.

Somehow, between the limp, staggering Doug and her own determination, she got him upstairs, one step at a time. She got his clothes stripped off him. She mopped him off with a few of Bunny's best towels and managed to tip him into Bunny's bed. She pulled the covers up to his chin.

"You're an angel," he got out.

"Go to sleep," she snapped. Feeling a big wet mass, she looked down.

Bingo stood right beside her, leaning against her leg, whining softly.

"Bingo, you are as wet as a wet rat!" She took him downstairs and spent a good forty-five minutes drying him off, repairing the damage he'd done to the downstairs—"But you couldn't help it, Bingo, you're a good boy," she assured him—and drying herself off. She changed into dry clothes that she tiptoed back into Bunny's bedroom to retrieve. Doug was snoring.

She stared down at him. "Doug," she said, exasperated. She realized she had said it out loud. But it would take cannonfire to wake Doug now, and he didn't stir.

She couldn't help herself. She reached over and smoothed a damp strand of hair off Doug's forehead, and felt herself softening.

"Nonsense," she said to herself. Out loud again, so she was feeling a little crazy. "You've just behaved like a prime jerk. You scared the crap out of me, and now I'm mad as hell," she told his inert form.

After a moment, she left him to go down to the kitchen, where she made herself a cup of herbal tea. She sat at Bunny's kitchen table, nursing it.

The temperature must have dropped ten degrees, and she felt chilled, so she grabbed one of Bunny's throws and pulled it around herself.

She thought about what Doug had done. He'd been very foolish. But as she took mental inventory of everything she knew about him, she realized his actions were completely out of character. "So what was that all about?" she asked herself. Then shook her head. Lunatic, she told herself. Still talking to yourself.

She couldn't stop thinking about it, though. What did his behavior mean? Why had he ended up on Bunny's front porch, drunk, in a rain squall?

The wind outside was still rising, and the sea was pounding at the shore.

Somehow, the fury outside Bunny's house gave her a cozy, safe feeling as she settled down on Bunny's living room couch to try to get some sleep. But the Doug situation unsettled her deeply, so for a long time she stayed awake, staring into the dark and listening to the storm.

Not the least of her unease? The eyeful she'd gotten of Doug's long, naked form as she stripped the wet things off him. The dim light from the upstairs hall illuminating him as she tucked the covers around him. How angry she was at him, how beautiful and vulnerable he looked, how much she wanted him, how much she wanted to rage at him. Part of her rage was how abominably he had behaved. But part of it. . .she faced herself in the dark. . .was how much she wanted to touch him, to make love to him, for him to make love to her, and how much she knew she could do no such thing or let him think any such thoughts about her.

Bright sunlight streaming through Bunny's plantation blinds waked her. That and Bingo's damp nose and thumping tail.

The storm had moved inland, leaving the air unusually clear and crisp for the time of year.

Gina unwound herself from Bunny's throw, all in a tangle around her, and stood up groggily, trying to shrug out a crick in her neck from sleeping crumpled up on the couch. "Come on, Bingo."

She was still in the dry clothes she had found last night. She searched for her shoes and the leash, and took Bingo out to do his business.

Coming back into the house, she petted Bingo absent-mindedly. "Good dog." She poured some kibble into his bowl, some fresh water into his dish, thinking hard. In a minute she heard his nails clicking on the stairs.

Gina followed him up. Doug, she knew, was passed out in Bunny's bed. Or maybe by now he was awake.

She needed to have it out with him.

When she cracked the door to look in, she saw Doug sitting on the edge of the bed, his head hanging. Beside him, Bingo was nuzzling under his hand to be petted. Doug looked up at Gina.

"Come on in. I'm decent," he croaked out. He'd wrapped the covers around his lower torso. He reached down to tousle Bingo's ears.

Gingerly, she stepped into the room, trying not to look at his lean body, the broad shoulders, the well-defined abs. If she looked, she was afraid she wouldn't be able to stop looking.

"So," he said after a moment, licking dry lips. "How mad at me are you?"

"Pretty mad," she said, but her words, instead of coming out stern, came out soft. Drat you, Gina Prine, she said to herself.

"I don't remember that last part of the night very well. I just remember trying to get into Bunny's house and falling down on her porch, and then I remember you being there. And I don't know how you did it, but you got me into bed. Thanks."

"What were you doing, trying to get into Bunny's house in the middle of a storm?"

"Looking for you, I think."

"You think?"

"Yeah. I knew you were staying here for the week. Theo told me. So that must have been what I was doing."

"Doug—" she began.

He waved a weary hand in her direction. "I'm sorry, Gina. I really am. When I was young and crazy, I had a couple of drunken incidents. None for years. Decades."

"So why now? Why this?"

"It's complicated."

"Okay," said Gina carefully.

"Okay, right now? Right now I'm about to throw up," said Doug, lurching off the bed and making for Bunny's bathroom, the covers trailing away after him. Bingo skittered out of his way.

Gina averted her eyes.

Retching sounds came from the bathroom.

After they had eased up, she called in. "When you feel a little better, come down to the kitchen and I'll make you something."

That seemed to trigger a round of fresh retching, so she left the room, closing the door behind her.

"Come on, Bingo." The dog reluctantly followed her. "You're worried about him too, huh?" she said to Bingo. In the kitchen, she made herself coffee and ate a bowl of cereal.

A while later, she heard feet clumping down the stairs.

"In here," she called out.

He hovered in the kitchen doorway, looking ashamed. "I feel better. I took a shower. But—"

She had to bite her lip not to laugh. He was wrapped toga-style in one of Bunny's sheets.

But he's not amusing. He's not cute. This is not cute, she scolded herself.

"Your clothes got soaked last night. They're in the dryer. Give them twenty minutes or so and you can put them back on."

"Thanks."

"Oh, and—" She thrust a tall glass at him. Bunny's patented hangover cure, o.j., raw egg, Worchestershire sauce.

Doug turned pale.

"Down the hall, to the left," she said urgently.

He turned and darted for the downstairs bathroom.

When he returned some time later, she held his clothes out to him.

He took them, whisked into the hall with them. She heard him hopping into his jeans. He edged back into the kitchen, pulling his tee over his head.

She tried not to gawk at how tight it was, how well it defined his abs. She looked levelly into his face. "Feeling better?"

"Yeah, but I don't think I can eat. . .drink. . .that." He nodded at the tall glass, which she had put on the side of the sink. He looked away from it quickly, and she saw him swallow hard.

"Coffee?"

"Yeah. Please. Black."

She poured him a cup, and he sagged down at Bunny's dainty kitchen table, a café table for two with matching fragile little wire-backed chairs.

"This house," he said. "I'll break stuff."

"Don't," she said, pouring herself a fresh cup and sitting down opposite him. "Want to tell me what the fuck you were doing last night?"

"I was going on a bender and acting stupid."

"Because?"

He sighed heavily. "I have a lot of problems."

She wanted to snap at him, so, what, add alcohol poisoning to the list? But she didn't. What was she, his mother?

"I shouldn't be here, Gina. The second the brakes were off the rational side of my brain, though—where did I come? Over here. Because you were here."

"And we both know why you shouldn't be here."

"Yeah, and now it's worse."

"You told me your divorce was only, what, weeks away? A month? Did you come over here to tell me you'd lied about that?" Because I know you did, she finished silently. A bitter silence settled about her.

"I didn't lie about it. I was blindsided. By Jaclin. She's my wife."

"We've met," said Gina drily.

"So I came to understand. I was in England when that ridiculous parking lot incident happened. Theo waited for me to get back before he told me. Believe me, Gina, I hated it when I heard Jaclin had pulled her Mean Girl act on you. And from what I hear, she even has a Mean Girl ally here in town. That realtor woman. Not the real one. The sub."

"Yes. I know," said Gina.

"You knew about her. The sub. Didn't you. That time we were over at the golf course home site, and she came instead of the regular woman, you stayed in the car."

"Yep. I've never liked her, and the feeling is mutual."

"In some ways, I think Jaclin has never left high school. Mentally."

Gina laughed. She knew. God, did she know the high school Mean Girls and the high school Queen Bees. Not many of them took art, and she thanked her lucky stars for it.

"I couldn't figure it out, why Jaclin had suddenly changed her tune about the divorce. When I left, she wanted it. Besides, I had. . .well, I had information that showed she was unfaithful, let's leave it at that. So that meant I should have had an easy time of it, getting that divorce."

"Something changed while you were away," Gina prompted, when it didn't seem like he'd be able to go on. Part of her wanted to say to him, don't tell me any more of it. You're a married man. I knew that. Let's just call it even between us. You leave, and we'll pretend none of this...whatever it is... ever happened.

But part of her wanted, desperately, to understand.

Doug groped around in his jeans pockets and came out with a creased, folded piece of paper.

"Oh. That went through the dryer, I'm afraid," said Gina.

Doug smoothed it out on the table between them. A photograph. It was much the worse for its spin in the dryer, but Gina could still make out what it showed. A taxi, and what looked to be a family that had just stepped out of the taxi, because several pieces of luggage were piled at their feet. Standing beside them, smiling into the camera, a very lovely blonde woman.

"That's Jaclin," said Gina, tapping the photo. "I recognize her. Who are these other people?" There was a tall young man who looked like he was maybe in his thirties. A pleasant woman. A little boy, really cute, too.

"That man." Doug pointed. "His name is John Richards. He's my son. And the woman is his wife. And the little boy is my grandson Ruan."

Gina said nothing, although she knew her mouth was making a round o of surprise.

"Complications," said Doug heavily. "I didn't know I had a son. I met this man in England. He says he's my son, and I believe him. Believed him. But now. Somehow now Jaclin has him."

Gina couldn't say anything for a minute. Finally she summoned up a question. "He's your son, but he's not Jaclin's?"

"That's right. At least I think it is. That he's mine." He took a breath. "He's sure not Jaclin's son. We didn't have kids. Jaclin didn't want any. Said they'd spoil her figure."

"You say Jaclin has him? What do you mean? Has him how? He's not a prisoner."

"No. But she has him. And she's going to use him."

"I see," said Gina carefully, although she didn't. The whole thing sounded crazy to her, and impossibly murky. But the look on Doug's face was so heartbreaking she couldn't stand to ask him more.

He stood. "I should go."

Gina followed him to the door.

"Thanks for last night," he turned to say, while she was stumbling through something like "I was so worried," she didn't quite know what. Her mind was all in a muddle.

They bumped together at the front door.

She found she had put her hand up to his face, just to touch him there, he looked so vulnerable, but instead her arms went around his neck, pulling his face down to hers, and she found herself kissing him.

And he was kissing her back.

They stumbled together into Bunny's living room and sank down on her couch.

"Doug!" she heard herself saying.

His hands were cupping her face and he was devouring her with his eyes. He ran a finger down her cheek, to her lips, and touched them gently. He ran his finger down the column of her neck to the little crevice at the top of her blouse.

She found herself undoing the buttons, one by one.

He moved his hands to her shoulders, gently pushing her blouse off, and then around to her back, fumbling with the bra strap.

She found herself helping him with the hooks.

And her hands, moving to the metal button on his jeans.

And he was helping her unbutton it, then unzipping his fly.

He stopped to lower his head to her breasts, circling each nipple with his tongue, gently biting down with his teeth as she drew in a gasp. And his hands to the waistband of her shorts. She helped him ease her out of them. She kicked her underpants into a corner.

Now with one hand he cradled the back of her head, pulling her face to his, putting his lips to hers, exploring her mouth with his tongue. Kissing her deeply, while, with his other hand, he began caressing her mound and moving to part her moist flesh with his fingers.

He stopped. Pulled back. "I want this. Do you want this, Gina? Do you?"

She couldn't tear her gaze from his, just grabbed his hand and moved it back to the place where his fingers were teasing her to a tingling need. "Don't stop," she whispered.

"Right here?"

"Right there."

"Oh, god, Gina, do I have anything?" he said, suddenly stopping. Reddening.

She looked at him uncomprehending. Then she realized. Condom, she thought blankly.

"I sure don't. Do I even remember how to do this?" she said. Condoms. Older lovers needed them too. She knew that. "Oh," she said, dismayed.

"Dammit, I don't have anything. But look. Let's just. ." He tilted her backward onto the couch, kneeling half on, half off it, burying his head between her thighs, while she sighed. Her back arched, doing so by itself, because she was lost to the feeling of his mouth on her, his tongue probing her. She moaned. And then she went over, over some cliff of desire into territory she didn't ever remember visiting.

He lay with his face on her belly, stroking her as she came in shuddering waves. They lay like that for a long time.

"God, you are the most beautiful thing I've ever seen, Gina Prine."

"This body has a lot of mileage on it, bud." She rose on one elbow and raised an eyebrow.

"I'd like to lick and nuzzle every mile of it, too." His voice was fervent.

She lay back, running languid fingers through his hair. She stroked the salt and pepper stubble of his cheeks. She didn't want to take her hands off him. She looked around to see where Bingo was. Bingo, tactful canine, had apparently gone off elsewhere for a nap.

After a moment, she sat up. Drank him in with her eyes, raked her gaze down his torso to his erect member, tight, engorged. Moved in on him. "Your turn."

Afterward, they lay facing each other and smiling.

"Guess it really is like riding a bicycle," she murmured sleepily, tucking herself into the crook of his arm. "You never forget how."

"Gina." He was nibbling at her earlobe. "I'd say you just won the Tour de France."

"Ha. I was thinking the Grand Prix."

"That's auto racing, Gina. Let's leave cycling out of it. How about the Ryder Cup?"

"Soccer?" she guessed. "Bowling?"

"You haven't known many jocks, have you, Gina?"

"Not Biblically, no. You're my first. I've led a sheltered life." And then, worn out as she was, not to mention deep-down satisfied, she fell asleep in his arms.

Fix it

DOUG COULDN'T STOP smiling. He also couldn't stop the small worm of worry that was eating itself up through the layers of content to the top of his mind.

He knew what he wanted. Gina Prine. But it seemed his life was conspiring to take it away from him. To take her away.

He hadn't told Gina the half of it, what he was facing with Jaclin and her shenanigans. The events that had led him so foolishly to get stinking drunk. The more he remembered of that, of what led him to his bad behavior, the darker his mood became.

Time to come clean to Theo. If anyone could make sense of it all, Theo could. Theo should be back today. He'd had to leave briefly to deal with some financial thing in Norfolk, but he was due back today.

Doug walked through the town, glad it was early on a weekend morning and not many people were stirring. By the time he got all the way down the highway to his house, his mood had sunk from euphoria to despair.

Theo was waiting for him as he limped up the walkway to the golf villa. And as Doug walked in, as he caught the first glimpse of Theo's expression, he realized, no, this was nothing Theo could fix. Maybe nobody could.

"Doug. I was about to call the cops. What the fuck."

"How long have you been back?'

"Drove back this morning. You left the door wide open. No one got in. That's a miracle and a half. Big storm, I get here, the door's open, the floors are all wet, and you are gone. I was thinking foul play until the next-door neighbor lady came over. You've heard the phrase Mad as a Hornet?"

Doug squinted his eyes against the light. It was hurting his head.

Theo plowed on. "Mrs. Soo was not gone five minutes than here comes the president of the club board. The earful I got from him? Hornets ain't in it."

"What did I do?"

"You, ah, misappropriated, shall we say, one of the club's golf carts and drove it across the newly-sodded eighth green. You'll be getting a bill for that, and it won't be cheap. And, I'm guessing, a stiffly worded letter from the club's board. By the way, I'm not sure what you did or said to Mrs. Soo, because she wouldn't tell me. Whatever it was, she did look ready to commit mayhem. Now that I think about it, judging from her expression, homicide really might have been a realistic possibility. Lucky you missed her visit. Honestly, Doug." Theo looked him up and down, taking in his disheveled state. "Do you need a nanny? Cause I ain't it."

"I was safe," said Doug, not meeting Theo's eye.

"Oh? And where did you go, may I ask."

"Don't ask, Theo," said Doug, looking up earnestly.

"No. You didn't."

"Yeah, I did."

"There's a self-destructive streak in you—"

"I know. I'm ashamed of myself. You don't have to say it."

"Are we talking spending the night at someone's house, someone I know and hope to protect just as much as I think you do? Someone both of us respect and love?"

"Not her house. Her friend's house. On the beach."

"Maybe no one saw you go in there."

"I don't think they did. It was storming." Doug found himself looking down again. "Someone might have spotted me as I left, though," he muttered.

"Dammit, Doug. Self-destruction's one thing, but destroying Gina. Now that's where I draw the line." Theo stood shaking his head, arms akimbo. He began to pace Doug's empty kitchen. "You WANT Mrs. Vindictive of the Year to take you to the cleaners? You want her to drag Gina into this? Cause if you do, keep it up."

"Oh, she's about to do that. Make no mistake about it."

"Howard is good at what he does."

"Yeah, but Jaclin is as underhanded as a snake."

"Snakes don't have hands, Doug."

"Look," said Doug, holding out the crumpled photo.

"That's—" Theo looked hard at the photo, clearly floored. "That's your son. And your grandson."

"And his wife."

"They're with Jaclin. What's going on, Doug?"

"Guess I'm about to find out. That photo was shoved under my door yesterday morning." Doug crinkled up his eyes again. He felt a massive headache coming on. "Or was that the day before? I've lost track. I might have to go to bed, Theo."

"You're too old for this kind of bullshit, if you don't mind my saying so," said his friend.

"You got that right."

"Okay. Good idea. Go to bed. You are looking pretty rough. But Doug. What do you make of this?" Theo flicked the photo with his finger. He handed it back.

"Well. My mind is working overtime on that question. I guess it could mean my son—or whoever he turns out to be—is in some kind of conspiracy with Jaclin to shake me down."

"Do you think she might try to put some deplorable construction on why you had never acknowledged your son?"

"I suppose that could be it. Is he even my son? He admitted he didn't find out about me through some DNA test. That he hadn't taken one."

"Too much of a stretch to think Jaclin hired somebody to pose as your son and meet you in England."

"Yeah, she doesn't have the imagination, one, and two, something like that would take cash she doesn't have."

"So somehow she found out about him and got to him. Does this photo suggest what I think it suggests? That he has flown over here with his family?"

"I was the one who gave him that idea. We were gonna get together over Facetime or Skype or whatever they have, and then if they wanted to, I was gonna send them tickets to fly over here."

"Looks like Jaclin beat you to it."

"Looks like it. I guess the big question I have." Doug closed his eyes briefly. "Is he here because he thinks I invited him? Because Jaclin made him think that, flim-flammed him into thinking she was a party to the invitation? I didn't talk over my marital woes with my son, you can bet I didn't, not when I'd just met him. Or did she and he plan it this way?"

"Makes no sense, Doug. What would she gain from something like that?"

"Make herself look like the good, warm, responsible party to our little divorce, and make me out the scoundrel."

"But why? Can't get blood from a turnip, bud. By now her shark lawyer must have broken it to her. Yeah, you won some nice prize money. But no, that kind of money won't keep rolling in. And no, you don't have some lucrative after-golf career lined up to keep her in the dough. All you really have is the golf course home, and as we see, Jaclin is jonesing after that. It's your one big asset."

Doug turned to the little shelf that ran along the divider between the golf villa's kitchen and its dining room. He plucked a fat envelope from it and handed it to Theo. "Read that. It might explain a lot. I'm going to bed." He turned back. "Uh. Theo. I think I may want to get a dog."

"You hate dogs."

"Pompom. And it's the reverse of what you think. Pompom hates me."

"Good lord, Doug. What DID happen to you while I was gone." Theo gave him the ghost of a smile. He looked aside at the envelope Doug had handed him. He pulled its contents out.

As Doug shut the bedroom door behind him, he heard Theo's soft exclamation.

"My god. Oh my god."

Yeah, thought Doug. Calling on the almighty might be the only thing left to do. But he doubted the almighty was interested in him and his misspent life.

Fix it yourself, loser, he imagined a higher power telling him.

And Bingo was his name

B. . .I. . .N. . .G, O," Gina sang softly, fondling Bingo's ears. Bingo sat lolling out his long pink tongue and loving it.

When Doug left, he had explained enough about the photograph of his son with his family that both of them realized the terrible truth. Doug and Gina had to stay away from each other.

"I want to come back, though," he told her, massaging her shoulders. "I want to come back properly equipped to love you the way you should be loved. You should always be loved, Gina. Only by me. Let me just add that part."

Gina giggled.

Remembering it now, she wanted to giggle again. But she also felt sad. The conflict with his wife would be over someday. It had to be. But how? And with what kind of outcome? She feared for him.

As he had turned to go, she had looked into the haunted gray of his eyes. "Take care of yourself," she said, her eyebrows creasing. She didn't want to be a nag, but after the stunt he had pulled, she was worried.

He knew what she meant. "I promise I'll never be so stupid again," he told her as he left. He glanced right and left off Bunny's porch. "And I'll make sure no one sees I've been here. I don't want gossip about you to come of my damnfool behavior."

But if he hadn't been that stupid, that much of a dumbass, Gina thought now, what would have happened between them? Nothing? Anything? Ever?

Whenever she thought of their blissful morning together, she had to stop to smile and hug herself. Then remind herself it couldn't happen again.

Today was sad in another way. "It's my last day with you, Bingo," she said, kissing the top of his soft head. "But you'll be glad to have your Bunny back, won't you, boy?"

At Bunny's name, Bingo perked up.

"Yeah. See? I'm sloppy seconds."

Bingo gave her a big sloppy dog-kiss with his long tongue.

"Awww, that makes me feel better." Then she and Bingo headed out for a long walk on the beach, the last one before Fran arrived from the airport with Bunny, and Gina returned to her own house. "I can come back and take you for walks," Gina promised into his ear.

Bingo wagged his tail furiously.

Once Gina was back to her own house, she got down to business. She had completely neglected it during the days at Bunny's, certainly the day of Doug's drunken appearance on Bunny's doorstep and beyond.

Three days of neglect. Three days not even looking at her email. Doing nothing about her projects. Three days didn't seem so long, until you actually had to face the pages of unanswered emails and the accusing pile of work.

Before she could get a good start on it, the ping from an incoming text accused her again: it was from Archer.

Driving through on my way to Norfolk. Dinner on Tuesday?

Gina hesitated. She was about to type no. She was about to conjure up some excuse. But instead she typed yes.

I've got to do it, she told herself. Thinking over past experiences, present-day hopes, she knew something about herself now. What Doug and she had, even so briefly, might be the best she could expect, maybe in her whole life.

As she thought about it, sure as the rains, she realized all over again: Doug and I can't be together. Certainly not any time soon. Maybe not ever. I need to see where this thing with Archer leads. I owe it to myself to see that.

As she whispered these words to herself, she knew they were actually Fran's words. Fran had given her a sensible talking-to on the way back to her house from her week at Bunny's. Fran had known something must have happened while Gina was supposedly primly house-and-dog-sitting, and Gina had half-confessed what it was.

And what do I want. Me? Gina? Another thought circling obsessively around and around the inside of her head.

By that time, she'd already typed in the yes to Archer's dinner invitation, and here came his very enthusiastic text back.

As Date Night approached, Fran and Bunny chivvied her into going back to Johanna and a trim and a freshen-up for the balayage. And now, as the Afternoon-Of was about to turn into Date Night itself, the two of them had shown up to approve the dress and the face.

"And there it is," said Gina, spotting Bunny's Adorable Me case.

"I like this dress," said Fran, examining what Gina had laid out on her bed to wear, an end-of-summer off the shoulders confection. "You've upped your game, girlfriend. This will show off your tan."

Bunny had laid her implements out on the kitchen table. She tapped the kitchen chair imperiously, and Gina sat down with a great show of obedience.

"The arming of the heroine," said Bunny, with a straight face.

And so it began.

This time, Gina ended up with hot-pink nails. "I match your car," Gina murmured.

"Where is he taking you?" said Fran.

"Elizabeth City, to that nice seafood place."

Fran and Bunny beamed their approval.

"Can we meet him?" Bunny blurted out.

"What, like the chaperones or the old aunties having to put their stamp of approval on the arranged marriage? No," said Gina.

"Marriage," said Fran, staring narrowly at Gina. She was awash in wedding preparations herself. "You think you'll say yes?"

"I don't know!" wailed Gina.

"You'll figure it out, girl," said Bunny. But she looked to be dragging her feet and getting ready to hang around. Fran determinedly towed Bunny and her case away.

"You owe me another pair of earrings," Bunny sang out as Fran bustled her into her car.

Archer arrived soon after. Gina found herself glad to see him. They headed out immediately for Elizabeth City in Archer's sporty Porsche.

As always, Archer's conversation was bright and witty. He handed her out of the car and into the charming little Elizabeth City restaurant. Ordered them drinks, appetizers.

Over the appetizers, some especially delicious calamari, not the rubbery kind, he stretched out his hand, smiling.

Gina put her hand in his. "Archer. . ."

"Don't say a word, Gina. I see my answer in your eyes," said Archer. "Those bright eyes of yours. You're breaking my heart, Gina, but I want my Gina to be happy and, well, if that's not going to be married to me, then, whatever else makes her happy, that is what I wish for her."

"Oh, Archer." Gina found herself tearing up. She dabbed at her eyes with her napkin. If her mascara ran, Bunny would be furious.

She'd gotten into Archer's car deciding she'd say yes to him. That it was the good and sensible thing to do. But by the time they'd pulled up at the restaurant, she knew her answer had to be no. The more she sat with her yes answer, the more wrong she felt about it.

"I don't understand it myself," she said. "I think you're great, Archer. Who wouldn't want to marry you? But I just."

"Can't," he finished for her.

The waiter was there at his elbow. He ordered a sumptuous feast for the two of them.

"There's someone else," he said, when the waiter had gone away.

She nodded, not trusting herself to speak.

"Lucky man."

She half-laughed, half-sobbed.

"Oh, now. You're not telling me the fellow isn't willing, are you?"

"No," said Gina, groping for words. She found some. Doug's words. "There are complications. I'm not even sure I want to marry this man, not even sure he wants to marry me. I just know I'm spoiled for anyone else."

Archer shook his head. "I am jealous as hell it's not me."

The wine steward came by. "Wine? They have a great selection. Oh, come on," he said, seeing her hesitate. "I'm driving, and after our one drink, I'm finished for the night."

She smiled gratefully and ordered a white.

"That will go great with the crab cakes. Wait'll you taste these beauties."

They were delectable. When Gina thought of ordering crab cakes, she nearly always thought better. They were nearly always heavily breaded and disappointing. But these were melt-in-the-mouth amazing.

At the end of the meal, he ordered an aperitif for her, a raspberry parfait for himself.

"That was wonderful, Archer."

"I have to treat my best artist right," he told her.

She looked across the table at him, troubled.

"Still thinking your presence in my galleries might be contingent on your answer to my little question? Pshaw, woman. Have some confidence in yourself. Your jewelry is a real draw for my galleries. A real boost to my business. It would have been nice to keep it in the family. But since I can't, I'll just keep on taking on whatever you can make for me, as fast as you can get it to me."

"What's wrong with me, that I can't say yes to your question, Archer?"

He waited courteously for her to get together her things and prepared to escort her back to his car.

"What's wrong? I'll tell you what's wrong," he said, steering her past the other diners.

Gina had barely noticed them, so intent had she been on Archer's question and then, once she had relaxed, the wonderful food.

"Did I ever tell you I'm kind of a witch, Gina? Like I have. . ." His eyes twinkled. ". . powers?"

"No, I don't think you've ever told me that," she murmured.

"Well, I do, and my powers tell me that the man sitting at the table across from us, with his friend, I guess, the man who has been scowling at me all night, might be what's wrong."

Oh, no. Gina looked around startled. To meet the gray eyes of Doug McNally, not ten feet away. Doug, who had started to rise to his feet. Theo was the man with him, putting a hand on his arm, saying something urgent to him. Doug sat back down, looked away.

Archer ushered her out to his car and got her settled in it. He swung into the driver's side and started the engine, which purred as if it had a beast under the hood.

As they sped back up the highway to the coast, Archer gave her a swift look. "I'm right, aren't I?"

"Yes," she whispered.

"I always am. I should set up shop and do seances."

When he said good night to her under her front porch light, he bent down and kissed her on the top of the head. "I hope it works out for you, Gina Prine. I don't want my artists unhappy. Bad for business."

Gina waved goodbye and let herself into her house. Dead tired, she sank down on her old comfy couch to kick off her heels and massage her arches.

Doug, she kept thinking, with fresh astonishment. Why had Doug been there? Was Doug psychic, too? Or was the whole thing some colossal, unhappy coincidence?

"Coincidence," said Fran briskly. "This is a small community with not much to do. You want fine dining, you go to Elizabeth

City. And where do you go in Elizabeth City? That seafood place, or Coastal Steak House."

"Stalking," said Bunny with a fierce little bob of her head. "That man is stalking you."

"I thought you were on Team Doug," said Gina, shakily.

They were in their booth at The Mermaid. Paula came by to take their orders.

After she was gone, Bunny made a little grimace and looked away.

"You're just mad because I left a big wet splotch on your lovely upholstery. I'm so sorry, Bunny. I used that stuff on it, the stuff you get at the hardware store. I should never have taken a bowl of soup over to the couch with me while I watched tv."

Bunny threw back her head and laughed. "You are such a bad liar, Gina Prine. No worries, I turned the cushion."

Gina blushed to her eyeballs.

"Anyway," said Bunny. "I am on Team Doug. I think what he did was sexy."

"Stalking is never sexy," said Fran, fixing Bunny with a severe look.

"He's not a stalker," said Gina. "And hush. The Vampire Queen just walked in."

The three studiously looked away as Amelia Gardner paraded past. For her part, she pretended they weren't there.

Gina suppressed an attack of nervous giggles.

Fran was not amused. "She doesn't like you, Gina, and one look at her, when she looks at you, tells me she'll do everything she can to make things go wrong for you."

"What did I ever do to her?" said Gina.

"Mess with her precious JoJo," said Bunny.

Gina heaved a sigh. "Yep. You're right. That's it."

"And no spoiled brat deserved it more," said Bunny. She rolled her eyes. "They're clients of mine."

Gina and Fran both cried out at the injustice of it.

"Business is business," said Bunny. "And mine is just getting off the ground."

"Paint her nails a putrid green," suggested Fran.

"Itch powder in her powder?" Gina. "Hemorrhoid cream in her lipstick?"

"Hemorrhoid cream?" they said, looking at her as if she had lost her mind. Then Fran got it and nodded. "Yeah, because when her mouth puckers up like that, it looks like an—"

"What are we, middle schoolers?" Bunny glared at them both, and they had to giggle again.

Gina went back with Bunny after they paid up and left. She had taken to borrowing Bingo. Long walks on the beach with Bingo. Just what she needed. Just what eased her sore heart.

She and Bingo headed off with Bunny's heartfelt thanks. Bunny had to get over to the little place she was calling her atelier to meet with yet another new client.

"I'd say your business is taking off," Gina told her. "Come on, Bingo. Let's get out of Momma Bunny's hair."

Gina scuffed along the beach, thinking hard. Mostly about Doug. About how his eyes had looked when hers met his at the restaurant. About how he probably thought she had abandoned him for Archer, and right away, too. Right after their morning together. How could she make him understand?

But why did he deserve to understand? He didn't own her. They had agreed, they couldn't see each other any more. What was she supposed to do, stay home?

But all her thoughts weren't about Doug. She was thinking about the start of school. Thinking about her finances. She came to a decision, and then she felt better.

"This is gonna be my last year as a high school art teacher, Bingo. I'm gonna turn in my resignation, and I'm gonna live on my art."

Bingo wriggled all over.

"Okay, boy. Want off the leash?"

Bingo shot into the surf, leaping joyously. Gina watched him with envy.

He came out and shook himself all over while Gina jumped back, laughing.

Then he took off up the beach.

There were only a few people far up the beach, walking. It was okay. Bingo would zip back to her in a few minutes. He was a very polite and astute animal. He knew not to bother any of the other walkers.

Except. Gina shaded her eyes. Damn. He was circling another beach-goer. Circling the man and barking.

"Bingo!" she called out.

But as she neared the man, her steps slowed. It was Doug. He was bending down petting Bingo.

When she got to them with the leash, he looked up at her, his gray eyes as clear and cloudless as the skies over a wintry beach. And just as chilly.

"Hello, Gina," he said.

Undue influence

THEO AND DOUG WERE cruising the Humane Society cages.

"Cute, but no," said Doug.

"This one's pretty cool," said Theo, pointing.

"Uh. Cool. Yeah. But no."

"Doug, we've looked over every pup the place has rescued. No," he shook his head at the attendant. "Sorry, ma'am, we can't make up our minds." Out in the parking lot, as they prepared to get into Theo's rental, Theo sighed. "Doug, you have this ideal dog in your head, and of course none of these dogs will ever measure up."

"Yeah," said Doug.

"Bingo is one of a kind, Doug."

"Yeah," said Doug.

"Want to drive to the next county, take a look at the Humane Society there?"

"No. I think I've had it for today."

"The real trouble's Gina. Isn't it." Theo pulled out onto the highway to head back to the golf community.

"Yeah."

"You need to get her out of your head, bud."

"I know."

"You've got other problems. Other fish to fry. Other kits in the kaboodle."

"Yeah."

"Talkative today, aren't we."

Doug said nothing.

"Any word from your son?"

"I've texted. Called. Emailed. Nothing. He may have blocked me."

"When we get back to my place, I think we need to strategize. And then I think we need to talk to Howard."

"Yeah."

"Especially about your dad. The thing with your son is just weird. The thing with your dad? Criminal."

Howard agreed, once they got him on Skype. "Okay, Doug, let's see if I've got this straight. You received a letter from your father with a new will."

"That's right."

"Notarized. Official."

"Yes."

"In the new will, your dad's longstanding bequest to the Northern Virginia Tennis and Social Club has been removed. You are the big beneficiary, and your brother still gets a pittance."

"Yeah."

"Have you had any interactions with your father lately?"

"None at all, not since I got back from England. That's when Theo and I visited him at Carolina Gardens and tried to get him to sign the power of attorney."

"And at that time"—here Howard steepled his fingers together and leaned in toward the screen—"He showed no signs of wanting to change his will."

"No, it didn't come up at all. He just ranted about how I wanted to take away his humanity, and how he wouldn't sign the power of attorney, and how his creditors could go fuck themselves, and how I'd never see a penny of his money. Just. . .Dad as usual." Doug thought about it. "No, wait. He accused me of wanting the power of attorney so I could take all his money. There was so much craziness, it's hard to remember it all."

"In the original will, he did arrange for you to get something," said Howard.

"Yes, some small bequest, and the same amount to Stan. Nothing new there. He's been crowing about it since we were teenagers. He says the reason he's leaving us anything at all is so's we can't go trying to break the will after he's gone."

"The dementia getting worse?"

"Seemed so. The doctors said so, when I met with them. But the will, Howard. The real one. This one I just got, it's a fake, Howard. Dad wrote that first will a long time ago, and he has been reveling in it ever since. He might have gotten a little crazier, but that part has never changed. A fine way to torture his sons beyond the grave, and he loves it."

"So what changed his mind?"

"I don't know," said Doug. Then, slowly, "but I can guess."

Howard waited.

"Jaclin. I'll bet she has been up there. And she is slow-walking this divorce thing, and trying to stop it entirely. We know that for sure. So—why would she? That's the question we've all been asking. Jaclin knows there's a lot of money in my family. It's just all tied up. She has always known that. She's known since Day One that I wouldn't inherit much of it. But suppose Dad changes his will? Suppose suddenly I'm the one who will get it all. The reason I'm pretty sure it's Jaclin. . .I mean, if Dad had suddenly seen the light and had decided he wanted to leave his loot to his sons after all, wouldn't he have split it evenly between me and Stan?"

"Maybe," said Howard. "You know, if Jaclin has been up there talking to him, and if she somehow persuaded him to change his will, that's a crime. It's undue influence of a vulnerable adult. It's elder abuse. North Carolina has laws against that. It's complicated to bring an action, though."

"If anyone tries to nail her on it," Theo put in, "Jaclin has the perfect fall guy. Doug. Who benefits? Doug, or so it seems. She might even think Doug won't try to go after her, because he'll see how much he stands to gain."

"She's wrong about that one," said Doug, scowling.

"Let's find out if Jaclin has been up there," said Howard. "You're in the best position to do that, Doug."

"I'll put a call in today."

"About the other thing."

"My son," said Doug.

"Yes. Now, you've told me how you met this man, this John Richards. The circumstances. And you've told me he admitted he hadn't taken any DNA test, just that his mother had always told him you were his father."

"Yes, and I believe him, Howard."

"I'd like him to take a DNA test."

"He said he didn't want anything from me. Why would he lie about it?"

"But he seems to be here in Charlotte with Jaclin. That's pretty strange, Doug."

"What's her game, Howard? What do you think?"

"Maybe to discredit you, Doug."

"That's what I think, too. I've tried calling John, but I think my number must be blocked."

"You think he blocked you?"

"I wonder."

"Let's work on the part with your dad first, Doug," said Howard before he signed off. "Fax the new will to me, would you? I'll take a look. Then we should get going on it. You can file a motion on behalf of your father. You'll need to get the nursing home docs, or maybe his personal physician, to certify that your father has dementia, so that's the part you should work on first."

"Will do. Thanks, Howard."

As Doug was about to end the call, Howard stopped him. "One more thing. I think it's pretty significant. My colleague Sarah, Jaclin's divorce lawyer? She has resigned the case."

"Huh?" said Doug.

"That tells me something illegal or maybe highly unethical may be going on," said Howard. "Sarah's a fire-eater, but she's not a sleaze. Food for thought."

The call ended. Doug turned to Theo with a sigh. "A lot of paperwork in my future. A lot of forms to fill out. And one more really unpleasant phone call to make."

Theo nodded sympathetically; he knew.

"Can't put it off," Doug said. He picked up his phone again and punched in his brother's number.

"Stan," he said, when the man on the other end picked up. "It's your brother."

When he ended the call, he was white-faced and shaking. Theo, who had stepped outside to give him some privacy, shot him a concerned look when he came back into the kitchen.

"Stan is accusing me of setting it all up and trying to grab Dad's money for myself." Doug shook his head. "I'm pretty sure Stan was high. At least he wasn't in jail. He babbled on and on about his new band. It's as if he hadn't even heard what I said, about Dad.

Then, when I tried to bring up the will again and tell him what I was about to do, he turned vicious."

"He's led a hard life," said Theo only.

"If I had been there for him more, been there to stand up for him, maybe I could have—"

"If you had been there in that household more, Doug, you would have been abused as bad as Stan was. I'm glad you weren't."

"I'll never forgive that old bastard for what he did to Stan. Mom could have stopped it. She could have tried."

"Maybe she did," Theo said gently. "He could have been abusing her, too."

Doug thought about his ramrod straight mother with her disapproving mouth. Her hard eyes. He shook his head. "I don't know, Theo. For a long time, I was glad I'd never have kids, you know? But now. Strange, huh? Now I'm glad I have a son."

"About that," said Theo. "I've been doing some thinking, especially after what Howard told us about Jaclin's lawyer. I think it's really out of character for Jaclin to do all the things we think she's doing. Doesn't that bother you?"

"Yeah. Eternal Mean Girl she is. Criminal mastermind she's not."

Around that time, the doorbell rang.

"Expecting anyone?" said Theo.

"I don't even know my neighbors yet. Except for that lady next door." Doug gave a little shudder. "Maybe it's her, serving me some kind of warrant or something for that thing I said to her." He headed for the front door. "Can you call the law on a drunk-out-of-his-mind asshole who calls his neighbor a bitch? Did I do anything worse? Did I pee in her pansies?"

Before Theo could answer, Doug reappeared, leading a tall young man. "Theo!" He was beaming. "This is my son John."

Get a life

SUNDAY NIGHT, AND GINA was sitting on Bunny's front porch steps and stroking Bingo's silky ears. They'd had a good walk. It was time for Gina to go home.

"Last day of summer, Bingo. This time tomorrow, I won't be able to take you on walks. Not so easily. I'll be really busy, the days will be getting shorter," she told him.

Bingo cocked his head, listening hard. He whined softly at her distress. Gina knew he understood her. Maybe not the exact words, but he got the gist.

She wanted a dog so bad. A dog just like Bingo. "But there's no dog just like you, Bingo," she said, nuzzling into the fur of his neck.

She thought about the avalanche about to descend on her and bury her.

This is why I can't have a dog. Exactly why, she thought. Right now, I have time to come over to Bunny's house and play with Bingo on the beach. Tomorrow, I'll have no time at all for anything but work. School. And work on my projects. All of it will come barreling down on me.

She was way behind on her projects. She owed Archer a ton of pieces. She needed to get special orders out, the ones that had come in from people who had seen her jewelry at the summer crafts fairs and had taken her business card.

But she couldn't short her students. That was set in stone. She never had and she had promised herself she never would.

The next day, the teacher workshops would begin. The week after, school would start, and the new crop of students would fill her classes.

On Monday morning, she loaded up her car with the plastic bins containing the art supplies she planned to use with her students. The school sure as hell wasn't going to provide them. They didn't have the money. She pulled into the teacher parking lot at Zebulon B. Vance High.

As she joined the herd of teachers streaming into the entrance that led to the teachers' lounge, she noticed many looked concerned or were exchanging worried looks with each other.

What fresh hell is this? she thought. Always something stirring up her colleagues, especially these days.

Before she could ask anyone, the principal strode in and lifted his hand for silence. Every teacher sat down on the sofas and chairs or on the sofas' arms, or leaned against the wall to listen. Every one of them could tell from their principal's expression. Clark Nubbins was not the bearer of good news.

"I want to say welcome to the new school year and blah, blah, blah," he began.

Already Gina knew what he was about to tell them was going to mean trouble. He never spoke like that. He was a smooth customer, and he used his talents on them, the parents, the school board, always to good effect. He'd been head coach of the football team for twenty years, and when he got boosted to principal, he knew his community well. Knew what they needed to hear and how to deliver his message.

But this. Gina could see the man was visibly shaken. She exchanged raised eyebrows with Marvin Pugh, sitting next to her.

"Okay, no way to say this but just blurt it out," said Clark Nubbins. "I've just gotten word of extensive state-wide budget cuts. This comes down to us from the State Legislature, and it sure ties my hands. It's going to gut us here at Zebulon B. Vance, and not just here. K-12 is hurting across the state."

As he talked on, the murmur of talk around Gina got louder and louder.

"Look, people. I'm gonna suspend our opening workshops. I'm gonna go into my office, and I want to speak to each one of you individually. This affects some of you more than others, and I want to talk to each of you mano a mano." No wussy gender-neutral language for Coach Nubbins. "It's gonna kick some of you in the balls, I won't lie. So I'm heading to my office now, and if you'll see Sally, here—" He nodded to his assistant, standing beside him with a clipboard. "—she's assigned each of you a number, and I'll see you in order." He turned on his heel and left the lounge.

The murmur became exclamations of outrage and fear.

"Some of us are about to lose our jobs, looks like," said Gina to Marvin.

"Looks like it."

"I'm guessing you guys in English will be okay. We know where all the first cuts always come. The arts." She gave him a wry smile.

"Yeah, I guess. I have tenure. Maybe they can still mess with me in a financial emergency. Guess I'll find out," said Marvin. "We've all got seniority, in our department. All but—" His eyes roved to the new person in their department, hired just the year before.

Gina nodded sympathetically.

"I hear you, about the arts. You don't look too worried, though." He gave her a quick puzzled glance.

Before she could answer, he waved his little paper in the air. "That's my number. Good luck, Gina. Time for me to face the Big Bad."

The name certain faculty members gave Clark Nubbins.

His supporters almost always referred to him as Coach.

All that trivial school politicking and bickering and drama, all the turf wars, Gina thought, were about to be revealed as the silly time-wasters they always had been. Get A Life syndrome, she thought with a cynical twist of her lips.

Her own turn came late in the afternoon. So there will be fewer people around to watch me get escorted from the building, she supposed. She noticed a lot of the people yet to have their turn with Principal Nubbins were in educational fields that didn't get much respect from some administrators.

She had also watched some of her colleagues hauling big boxes out to the parking lot. Several of them were crying.

She sat around all day, fiddling with her phone, trying and failing to sketch out some ideas for new pieces. Now Sally the Administrative Assistant summoned her from the doorway.

She hauled herself to her feet and followed Sally. Sent to the principal's office! Gina almost laughed.

"You can go in now, Ms. Prine," said Sally softly, her eyes sympathetic.

"Hi, Clark," she said as she entered.

He waved her to a seat in front of his desk, the suppliant before the monarch.

Gina seated herself. Before he could speak, she said, "Clark, I resign."

He gave her a level look. "Gina, don't. Lemme tell you I'm laying you off. Then you can collect all the benefits."

"Okay, then lay me off. I was going to make an appointment to tell you this would be my last year, anyway."

Clark grunted. "The arts always get it in the neck, am I right? Way I hear it, some art teacher's gonna travel around the district teaching mini-classes, but that's at the elementary level. At the high school level, we just can't afford it. Not with these new cuts. You understand."

But we can afford football just fine, thought Gina. "Oh, I do," she said instead.

"I've went to bat for you in previous years, Gina."

"Thank you for that, Clark." Too bad you didn't take your English classes very seriously, but not my problem.

"They've gone and moved the goalposts on me."

She nodded.

"Saw it coming oh, a year ago now. Tried a goal-line stand. I want you to know that. But they did an end-run around me."

"Not just you, I hear. Us," she amended. "I hear the whole state is affected.

"Yeah. A shame. Those pols, they play hardball for sure." He shook his head, looking doleful. "Called our state rep over the summer. He claimed there were things he could do to help. Guy bricked it." Nubbins looked down at his desk, where everything was neatly arranged and squared off. Pens. Ruler. She wondered what he needed a ruler for. Blotter tucked into leather corners. Then she realized. He had an entire little monogrammed desk set going on. "I'm glad you understand, Gina. It's gonna be a whole new ball game around here. Education-wise."

Gina rose to go. She felt sorry for him. He seemed genuinely miserable. "Thanks, Clark. I'll just get my things."

By the time she ferried her few belongings out to the parking lot—a sweater she'd forgotten to take home at the end of last year, stuff like that—she could hardly keep herself from whooping with joy. She was glad she hadn't lugged her art bins inside the building yet. Annoying enough to have to drag them out of the car once she got home. She'd have to sort through them, see what she could use in her own work, donate the rest somewhere. The church scout troop, maybe, or the Sunday School.

She was sorry about the students, though. She'd liked most of them. Loved a few. But she was going to have to face those feelings at the end of the year. May as well do it now, before she fell in love with a whole new crop.

She did have a sad moment later in the day, when Shari Morrison, one of her most talented students, rushed up to her in the canned goods aisle of the Food Lion and hugged her and cried on her.

But she and Bunny and Fran had agreed to meet for a quick supper at The Mermaid, to celebrate Gina's first day back at work, or maybe to commiserate, so she had that to look forward to.

She was the first there. Paula settled her into their usual booth and brought her iced tea to her. "Honey, I heard," Paula said, wet-eyed. "I'm so sorry."

"It will be fine, Paula. Really it will," said Gina. She didn't even have the heart to summon Paula back and remind her how much she hated sweet tea. She gulped it down.

Just as she spotted Fran in the doorway and started to wave her over, she heard voices filtering over from the next booth. That voice. Amelia Gardner's.

". . really, what do some of those teachers do all day, anyhow? Then they have all summer off. . . "

An indistinct murmur back.

"Fluff courses like art," Amelia was proclaiming. "And some of them, why, they just indoctrinate our children, is all. . ."

By then, Fran had reached their booth. She slid in beside Gina, shaking her head. She had overheard Amelia, too.

"You work all summer at other stuff," Fran bent closer to Gina to say, between gritted teeth. "You work because they don't pay you enough. And I see you with all those planning materials spread out across your kitchen table. You're thinking and planning for the school year all summer, too. You even buy most of your own supplies, and with your own money." Fran was waxing indignant.

Gina put a finger to her lips and shook her head, smiling.

After a moment, they both heard a rustling from the booth behind them. Amelia and one of her cronies emerged to stalk from the place into the parking lot.

Gina laughed. "Hey, and now I don't care what that woman thinks, because I never have to teach her rude kid again."

Paula showed up again to take Fran's order. She pushed a tall iced tea at Gina apologetically. "Sorry, hon, I was so upset I forgot."

"Thanks, Paula. I need to get fired every day. Everyone is so nice to me!"

"Carly was all signed up for your class. Now I guess she has to take keyboarding instead."

"A useful skill to have, though. Tell Carly I said hey," Gina told her

"How can you be so cheerful about it?" said Fran, when Paula had gone.

"The school has its new strat, right? Its new game plan, as Principal Nubbins calls it. Cut out the fluff, like art. Put in office skills like keyboarding."

"Talk about a gut course," Fran groused.

"Anyhow, I was about to resign."

"You were?" Fran was floored.

"Yeah. Concentrate completely on my business."

"You can make your jewelry pay well enough to replace your salary?"

"Uh—" Now the difficult part, thought Gina. "Well, I got an email from Archer over the weekend. He wants me to open a new gallery for him, and administrate it. Up in Highlands."

Fran's mouth gaped open. "But—" she faltered. "But you'll have to leave Currituck Cove. Leave the beach!"

"I know," said Gina. She shifted uncomfortably. The moment was saved by Bunny, who darted in and slid across from them.

"I'm late!" she proclaimed. "But guess what, I just got a new client, and she's from the golf community, too. Doug's neighbor, I take it." She cast a delicate look in Gina's direction.

"Not the one he—"

Bunny nodded. "Afraid so."

"Don't tell her you're on Team Doug. That's my advice."

"You know it, girlfriend. Keeping that to myself. So what's going on?" She looked from Gina to Fran. Caught their somber mood.

"Have you been hiding under a rock?" Fran shook her head at Bunny. "It's the Monday Morning Massacre. A full quarter of the teachers at the high school were laid off, and a lot of the remaining ones had their jobs cut or got reassigned to lower-paying positions."

"Or got their courseloads doubled, and their class sizes," said Gina.

"No!" said Bunny. Then she clapped her hand to her mouth. "Gina! Not you!"

"Tell her, Gina," said Fran, so Gina had to start all over again, explaining the whole thing to Bunny. Ending with Archer's plan to lure her away from the beach and up into the mountains.

"Do you think Archer has ulterior motives?" Fran wiggled her eyebrows.

"Nah," said Gina. "True, I'll be a lot closer to Charlotte, and Archer's main gallery, but further away from his ancestral domicile."

"That lovely house in Southport." Bunny sighed. "And it all could have been yours, Gina."

"I thought you were on Team Doug," said Gina in mock-outrage.

"Well, I was. Looks like that's not gonna work out, huh."

"Looks like it."

"Gina, I don't like it," Bunny mourned. "Fran's going off to be married. You're moving to the mountains. You two are abandoning me."

"Silly, I'll be in Elizabeth City. That's practically around the block," said Fran.

"And I haven't said I'm going to move to the mountains. Just that I'm thinking about it."

"Now, though," said Fran. "Now, unless you really think you can make a go of it on your jewelry alone, you'll have to get something else. And opportunities like Archer's don't just drop in your lap every day."

"Very true," said Gina. "I really had been thinking of trying to make a go of it with my jewelry alone. Like, taking early retirement and just doing art. I'd have to scale back, though, and could I make it work financially? But now, my bluff's been called."

"And Archer has ridden to the rescue," said Bunny.

"At least I can tell myself that Archer doesn't know that's what he's doing, rescuing me. I don't like thinking he is. No," she said, at the expressions of the other two. "Stop. I'm not marrying Archer. I'm not letting some man rescue me. I can take care of myself."

"But are you at least going to think about Archer's offer. The gallery, I mean?" said Fran.

"Yeah. I suppose I should." The three of them looked at each other glumly. Move away from the beach!

"The mountains are beautiful, though," said Gina, brightening. She sank back into gloom. "But my friends are here."

And, a little voice niggled at the back of her mind, Doug is here.

Go away! she said to it, shocked. After everything, you're still thinking about that guy?

What the heart wants. . . the little voice began.

Shut up, she told it firmly.

Meet the fam

DOUG INSISTED THAT John drive his family in from the outlying motel where they were staying. "This place has three bedrooms. I'm in one, Theo is in one, and you and Lila can stay in the third. Think we can make a bed on the floor with cushions and a quilt for little Ruan?" Lila, Doug had discovered, was John's wife.

"Ruan would fancy that," said John. "It will be like when we go on holiday to the seaside and we all pile into a twee caravan together." When Doug showed him the third bedroom, his eyes widened. "Quite a bit larger than the seaside caravan, innit," he murmured.

"Or," said Theo to Doug, "you could go down to the rental place to rent him a baby bed."

Ruan, it turned out, was too big for a baby bed and declared he was not a baby. Then he ran from room to room of Doug's house, leaping and yelling."

"He's a right angeltwitch, he is," said Lila to Doug, smiling shyly.

"He's an angel, all right," said Theo. "What a gorgeous little boy."

Once everyone had been introduced and Ruan had been given a juicebox, the adults went out onto Doug's brick patio to relax and get to know one another.

"I'm glad you found out how to get to me, John," said Doug. "I was really worried. Someone let me know you were in the States, but when I tried to call you, I could never get through."

John's face darkened. "Someone had taken my phone and blocked your number," he said.

"I thought something like that must have happened. I was worried you were the one who had blocked my number, John."

"No," said John.

Theo came out of the kitchen with iced teas and passed them around.

"Come on out here and sit down, Theo," said Doug, realizing Theo was hanging back. "Theo is my good friend from college, and he also manages my finances."

John and Theo shook hands.

"I don't want to intrude," said Theo. "This looks to be a ticklish family situation."

"You never intrude, Theo. Come on out here." Doug turned to his son. "John, I don't want to pressure you, but could you tell me a little bit about what's going on? I'm pretty confused."

John hesitated. Lila had no such qualms. "Mr. McNally, I think Mrs. McNally a bit daft."

"You can say that again."

"Dummon," said John under his breath.

Lila grinned and elbowed him in the ribs. "It's only true, John."

"We got your letter, and the air tickets for the three of us," John began.

"Wait. Wait. What? I didn't send you a letter."

John stared. "But the tickets—"

"And I didn't send tickets. I was going to, but I wanted to wait to see whether you did want to come, and when."

Lila was nodding. "Remember how strange it was, John?" She turned to Doug. "We thought you very generous, Mr. McNally. We'd been talking about buying the tickets ourselves, you see. We thought you shouldn't pay. But then, when they came in the mails that way, well, we thought we mustn't waste them, and we did want to come over."

"Your letter reassured us you really did want us, Mr McN—" John began.

"Please. Call me Doug. Or call me—no, too soon for that, I guess," he said to himself in an undertone. "Call me Doug." He looked at the couple, then down at his grandson, leaning against his mother's leg. "Little Ruan looks done in."

"Tuckered out. It's going on dimmit," said Lila. "I'll just pop him in his twee bed, shall I?" She hauled him away, his head lolling.

"John," said Doug urgently. "I'm afraid my wife Jaclin—soon to be my ex-wife, actually—has done something underhanded. That letter wasn't from me. The tickets weren't from me."

"We thought it strange, when we arrived in the States and Mrs. McNally met us, not you, sir," said John. "She explained you were off at a golf tournament and she had a nice place for us to stay until you returned."

"Where did you stay? Somewhere in Charlotte?"

"Yes, a very nice house. We had it all to ourselves." He described it.

"Uh-huh." Doug looked over at Theo. "Sounds like Mallie's house. My wife's friend," he explained to John. Privately he was making some quick calculations. Mallie was a flight attendant. Maybe that's how Jaclin got the tickets. Would she have really paid out of her own pocket, no matter how much she schemed, to fly three people from the UK to the US? Not full fare, anyhow. "My wife's friend travels a lot," he explained out loud, "and Jaclin has the key to her house. So then what? Weren't you worried when I never showed up?"

"Very," said John. "Each day, we got a bit more worried. Mrs. McNally came by, and she was very kind. Brought toys for Ruan. Took Lila shopping. But something was wrong. Lila and I felt it. Then she brought a man to see us."

"Oh?'

"Describe him," said Theo.

John did.

"Dammit," said Doug. "This is getting clearer. Sounds like Trey."

"This is not a friend? The man claimed to be your good friend, and he wanted to know all about us. How you and I met, how I found out you were my father. At first, Lila and I agreed you must be trying to make sure I really am who I say I am—"

Doug was getting angrier by the minute.

Theo put a hand out. "Ok, Doug. You have every right to be angry, but let's hear John out."

"So," said John quietly. "You didn't ask this man to check up on us. On me."

"No," Doug bit out. "I'm outraged anyone—Jaclin, that man—put you through such an experience."

"So then," said Theo. He stopped himself. "I hope you don't think I'm butting in here, John. As Doug has explained, I'm a friend, I handle Doug's financial affairs, and I'm in close contact with Doug's lawyer. I'll step outside if you want to talk to your father privately, though."

John was shaking his head no. "I have nothing to hide. I told Mr. McNally—Doug—from the first. I want nothing from him. I just wanted to meet my father."

"So," said Doug. "This man—his name is Trey Nichols—was probing you about who you are, how you and I met, things like that."

"Yes. And then he started suggesting things. That maybe you were taking advantage of me. That maybe you had kept things from me, deliberately hidden from me that you are my father. He suggested that maybe you had decided you didn't want to meet me after all, and that's why you hadn't come back to see us. He wanted me to talk to some lawyer he and Mrs. McNally knew. That's when I was sure something had gone very wrong."

Doug nodded. "Yes. And now here you are. You found me. I'm glad."

"How did you do that, John?" said Theo.

"It was so odd that Mr. McNally—Doug," he amended, casting a shy look at Doug— "hadn't even called me. Then I happened to take a hard look at my mobile, and I realized Doug's number had somehow been blocked. I hadn't done it. I'm afraid—I'm afraid Mrs. McNally might have gotten her hands on my phone."

"I'll bet she did," said Doug.

Lila had come back by then and plopped down onto the bench with her husband. "Ruan's fast asleep." She nudged her husband. "Yes, John, remember how odd it was. Mrs. McNally said she'd put in a number where you could reach her."

"She grabbed it out of my hands and started in on it," said John, shaking his head. "I was trying to explain to her how she could easily send her information from her own phone to mine, but she just grabbed it." John went on with his tale. "Once I had my suspicions and gave my phone a hard look, I saw your address in my contact list, where I'd put it in after we met in Devon. But that wasn't Mrs. McNally's address, the address on the letter we thought you had sent. It was the address for this place. Before we came over, we didn't know much about North Carolina. When I went to the Internet to look, I saw the address you gave me was many kilometers away from the place in Charlotte."

"We smelled a rat," Lila put in.

John squeezed her hand. "And then I noticed your number had got blocked somehow. Lila and I waited a bit, because Mrs. McNally told us she wasn't coming by for a few days, that she had things to do but hoped we'd be comfortable. We were. There's a pool. It's a very lovely house."

Lila turned to Doug. "Ruan loved the pool. But we knew something was wrong. So we looked up how to call a car, an Uber, I believe."

"Yes, and we made the driver take us to a rental car agency, and then we drove here."

"It's daft, you Yanks driving on the wrong side of the road," said Lila. "Fair terrified me."

"Did you tell Jaclin you were leaving? What did you say to her when you left?"

John and Lila looked at each other.

"Nothing," said John. "We decided if we didn't find you when we got to this town, we would call the police. And then we'd go home."

"I'm glad you found me. You two are very resourceful. A strange country, and you knew to get out of there."

"John works with the computers," said Lila. "He knows how to do anything."

Doug grinned. "Great wife you got there, John."

John smiled and took Lila's hand and squeezed it.

"Well," said Doug. "I think I can explain to you what's going on. It's not a pretty picture. I really apologize for that."

He was getting angry, and Theo saw that. "May I, Doug?" He turned to the others. "Doug's wife is trying to shake him down—er, trying to do something illegal to undermine their divorce," said Theo. "She thinks John has a lot of money, and she wants it. That man you met, Trey Nichols, we think is her accomplice."

"Shady," said John, with distaste.

"And maybe this Trey slimeball put her up to it," said Doug. "By the way, it's not at all true I have a lot of money. I mean, I do all right." He looked around at his property, the landscaping, everything. "Let's go in, before the mosquitoes eat us alive."

They all settled themselves in Doug's sparsely furnished living room.

At least there are beds in the spare rooms, thought Doug. Next month, another of the college crew, Alberto, the ex-quarterback, was coming by for a few weeks of late beach fun. Theo would have to go back to Chicago, although there was room for both, and he wished Theo could stay longer.

But now he picked up his conversation with his son where they'd left off. "Very shady," he agreed. "Criminal, even. But the very last thing I would ever want is for you to get mucked up in the whole sorry mess of my divorce, John. I was hoping not to even have to tell you about it until it was over. Not to even have you visit until it was over, although it has dragged out now. I mean, you took a big risk, telling me who you are. And this is the thanks you get?" He shook his head. "I'll buy tickets for you to get home. It would make me so happy, though, if you'd consider staying for a few days longer, so we can get to know one another."

In an undertone, Theo said, "Call Howard in the morning?"

"Yes, and after we hear Howard's advice, call the police."

Yard sale smack-down

"YOU'RE SURE ABOUT THIS?" said Fran, helping Gina tape a poster to a pole at the intersection of her street and the town's main drag.

YARD SALE TODAY!

"I'm sure. I'm putting the house on the market Monday," said Gina.

"But you haven't even decided for certain to move to the mountains," said Bunny, taping up a poster on the other side of the intersection.

"I know. But once I had decided to retire early, I knew I'd have to sell my house. I've already looked into it. Talked to a realtor."

"Not the one who works with Amelia Gardner, I hope," said Fran, stretching up on her toes with a big roll of tape.

"What am I, nuts? Of course not. I went to the other firm in town."

"She could still get involved," Fran warned. "If a buyer is using her, she could profit from your sale."

"Can't do anything about that, now, can I?" said Gina, sorting through her signs and deciding where else to post them.

"Anyway," she said, "the realtor told me it was a good time to sell. Prices are going up around here. Because of the golf community, I guess, and always because of the beach. This is a really modest little house, but my realtor says even little houses like this are doing well. He says my home value has almost doubled since I bought it ten years ago. So, sell out, and if I don't move to the mountains, I'll buy something much cheaper a lot further inland. Then I'll be able to afford my new reduced lifestyle."

"Makes sense," said Fran, grudgingly.

"Anyhow, whatever I was going to decide to do a year from now, I have to decide right away. The school board and state educational policy have taken the decision out of my hands."

"I guess," said Bunny, sighing. "But you think you'll move to the mountains?"

"I'm still not sure. I owe Archer an answer next week. I'll have to make up my mind fast."

After they finished putting up the poster, the three headed back to Gina's yard, where her former student Ada was holding down the fort before going to her job at the golf club. The three friends knew that though the sale was due to start at seven, true to yard sale form, all the biggest yard sale bargain hunters would be assembling well before.

Gina strode to the main card table she had set up, while Bunny whisked into her house to retrieve her box of change.

Gina smiled at the early comers, who were all looking antsy.

Bunny brought out the box.

"Okay, neighbors. Yard sale's open." Gina called out. With the help of her friends and Ada, she was selling, selling, selling. At last, close to eleven a.m., the shoppers had slowed to a trickle and the early fall sun was heating things up.

Gina wiped sweat off her forehead with the back of her hand. "Hey, I can take it from here," she told Bunny. Fran had long ago left for the bank. She looked over at Ada. "Ada, grab anything you like as my thanks for helping out."

Ada looked around at the picked over tables shyly.

"No, wait," said Gina. "Hold down the shop for a sec?"

"Sure, Ms. Prine."

"I'll be quick," said Gina. I know you have to go serve lunch at the club."

When she came back out, she'd found a pair of her prettiest earrings in the Celtic design she'd taken to the mountains, one of her best sellers. "Here," she said, pressing them into Ada's hands. "Something to remember me by."

"Wow, thanks, Ms. Prine! As if I could forget you. And oh, Ms. Prine?"

Gina raised her eyebrows. Ada looked flushed.

"Uh. Mr. McNally is here to see you. There he is, over there, with his friends."

Gina's eyes widened.

At the same time, Doug spotted her, and threaded through the nearly empty tables to her, trailed by . . .looked like Theo, of course, but who were those other people? A younger couple and a little boy.

Ada gave her a quick smile and darted for her bike.

"Gina," said Doug. He seemed a little out of breath.

"Hi, Doug."

"Uh, heard you were leaving town. Heard about the cuts at the high school. Shameful."

"I'd decided to leave anyway," said Gina, looking at him, wondering. The last time she'd encountered him, that time on the beach with Bingo, his expression told her he never wanted to set eyes on her again.

It had hurt. Badly. Gina tried to summon up a smile.

"Gina," he said, and swallowed hard. "I was wrong to behave the way I did last time I saw you. Wrong and selfish. I came by to wish you the very best, before you leave. I hear you're moving to the mountains."

"Maybe. It's not a done deal yet," she said.

"Away from here, anyway."

"Seems it's time."

"Gina. None of my business, but that man I saw you with, at the restaurant? That the one? The one taking you away from us?"

She saw what an effort it was for him to ask it. She wanted to snap, You're right, it isn't any of your business. Instead she said, "What a gossipy little place this is. That man, as you call him, is my new boss, Archer Deveraux. He owns several art galleries in the state. We were talking over dinner about his plans to open a new art gallery in the mountains. About whether I should go up to the mountains to run the gallery." Sort of a lie, she thought, with a twinge of guilt. The timing of it, anyway. Not much of one. "And I may do that." She ended on a frostier note than she'd meant.

"I see," he said, looking more miserable than before. "Wish things had ended better between us," he said softly.

"Well. There it is," she said briskly. She looked past him. "Hi, Theo. Good to see you back!"

"Hi, Gina."

She was about to turn aside, to start packing up the dregs of the yard sale, when Doug stopped her.

"Uh, Gina. I sort of hoped—"

"Yes?" Damn, that came out more unpleasant than she'd planned, too.

"I wanted to introduce you to some people."

"Oh. Sure."

Doug summoned the younger couple over. "This is John Richards and his wife Lila. They're from England."

"Devon," said the younger man, John. He held out his hand and Gina shook it.

His wife smiled at her.

"And who's this?" said Gina, suddenly remembering the people in the photo Doug had shown her.

"This is Ruan," said the woman, Lila. "Our son."

Gina crouched down at eye level. "Hi, Ruan!" She looked up. "What a beautiful child."

"Gina," said Doug, shifting uncomfortably. "I met John when I was playing golf over in England a few months back."

"Oh?"

"Uh, and he and I discovered, well, he's my son. You may remember the photo I showed you."

"Yes, I do remember that," she said. To the young man and his wife, she said, "How amazing. You hear about stuff like this happening, what with the DNA tests and all."

John looked like he was about to say something and then thought better of it. He just smiled.

"Will you stay over here long?" she asked him politely.

"We're heading back in the morning."

"You must be very happy to have your family here with you, Doug," she said, and meant it.

"I am." He reached down and tousled his grandson's hair.

At that moment, Bunny reappeared.

Ruan squealed.

"I forgot to get my—" Bunny began. She stopped.

Ruan made a rush for her.

Then Gina saw. Ruan was making a rush for Bingo, whom Bunny had on his leash.

The adults gazed down at dog and child, happily licking (dog) and patting (child).

Thanks, Bunny, thought Gina. That could have been an awkward moment. Instead, it was an aww moment.

"We have a dog at home. You miss Bananas, don't you, Ruan? We'll get on the plane, and you'll see Bananas soon."

"Bananas!" crowed Ruan.

"There was a dog at the house where we were staying in Charlotte," Gina heard Lila tell Doug. "Not a very nice dog, I'm afraid. He nipped Ruan."

And Doug's grim voice. "Oh. Pompom."

Into the midst of a fraught situation, as if it didn't need to get any fraughter, minced Amelia Gardner, one of her friends in tow.

"Oh," she said, looking over the remnants of the yard sale with distaste. "Guess we're too late for the good stuff. Come on, Connie." She spotted Doug then. Looked from Gina to Doug with a malicious little smile.

"Hello, Mrs. Gardner."

"Hello, Mr. McNally. I hope you're enjoying the condo."

"Very much so," said Doug. "But Mrs. Gardner. I understand you know my wife."

"Oh? Oh, yes, I think I met her during a rather uncomfortable incident in your parking lot. You were in England at the time, I believe, but all's well that ends well."

"Not sure that little incident has ended so well," said Doug.

Amelia looked, Gina thought, the least bit alarmed. "I don't know what you mean." Connie, her friend, was drinking in every word.

"No?" said Doug, rounding on Amelia. "Think about this, then. My lawyer let me know this morning that the Charlotte police have just arrested a man named Trey Nichols for fraud. A crime called fraudulent pretense. As soon as I see these good people off to the airport, I'm headed to Charlotte myself, where I'll decide whether I want the police to charge my wife with fraudulent pretense and elder abuse, because apparently she helped Trey Nichols do it. Hope you didn't play any part in . . ." he paused a good long while. Amelia Gardner's expression moved from alarmed to frightened. " . . . any of that," Doug ended softly.

Amelia Gardner collected herself. "I have no idea what you're talking about."

"No?" Doug smiled at her, not a very nice smile, Gina thought. "To be on the safe side? Get yourself a good lawyer, Mrs. Gardner."

Amelia Gardner and her friend hustled away.

What the—Gina was thinking.

Doug turned to his son and daughter-in-law. "Just when I think things have settled down and I start hoping you'll think your father is actually some normal guy, another incident out of a cheap reality tv show pops out. You'll never want to come back."

John put his hand on his father's arm. "We will," he promised.

Bunny was gathering in Bingo's leash. Ruan was looking heartbroken.

"Puppy!" he cried.

His mother swooped him up with promises of ice cream.

"Well," Gina said uncertainly. "Have a good flight back."

As they waved and made their way to Doug's car, parked on the street, Bunny reeled Bingo in. He wanted to go lolloping after Ruan. Bunny turned to Gina. "Girlfriend, everything is gonna be so boring when you leave. How will I stand it, without all the drama?"

"What just happened?" Gina whispered.

"I don't know and I don't care," said Bunny. "But I'll treasure the look on Amelia Gardner's face forever."

I concede

"NO," SAID DOUG, MAYBE more forcefully than necessary. "I want to be there. I want to look her in the eye."

"Very well, Doug," said Howard. "I recommend you let the lawyers handle this, but—" He threw up his hands. "Your choice."

Howard led the way to his conference room. Jaclin and her own lawyer were already seated across the conference room table. A different lawyer, not Sarah the shark. A criminal lawyer.

Doug stared at Jaclin until she dropped her eyes. He took a seat beside Howard.

"First off, my client Mr. McNally has every right to press charges against Mrs. McNally for participating in the crime of false pretense, and most heinously of all, for elder abuse," said Howard. "My assistant has just deposed Mrs. McNally's friend, a woman named Amelia Gardner, who was a party to some of Mrs. McNally's actions. Mrs. Gardner claims she didn't realize she was participating in a fraud, but she has agreed she will cooperate with the law."

Jaclin's lawyer said nothing, just made a note on the pad in front of him.

Jaclin gave Doug a piteous look, dabbing at her eyes, but Doug had seen Jaclin turn that look on and off at will over the years, and he was having none of it.

"Let me enumerate," said Howard. "Mrs. McNally fraudulently convinced various parties that she had the right to enter Mr. McNally's domicile, maintained separately from hers, and was stopped in the act of trying to destroy some of his property. Mrs. McNally's associate, Trey Nichols, under indictment for false pretense and elder abuse, has confessed Mrs. McNally's part in his crimes." Howard took a breath. He looked over at Doug to make sure, Doug surmised, that Doug was under control and doing okay.

Howard is right, Doug thought. I shouldn't be here. I'm too angry to be here. But I can't not be here.

Howard went on. "Mr. McNally's father, Joseph P. McNally, a resident at Carolina Forest, a nursing home in Raleigh, has been diagnosed with dementia. Mr. McNally knows of his diagnosis, and so does Mrs. McNally. Without Mr. McNally's permission or knowledge, Mrs. McNally went to Raleigh with Trey Nichols and Amelia Gardner. There she convinced the nursing home administration that she was a family member on a friendly visit to Mr. McNally senior. She was admitted. At that time, Trey Nichols has confessed, Mrs. McNally reassured Mr. McNally senior that she was there to help him, while Trey Nichols fraudulently obtained his signature on a will invalidating his old will. Amelia Gardner, a notary, then notarized it. Charges against Mrs. Gardner have not been pressed, since she has agreed to cooperate with the State of North Carolina's investigation into this act of fraudulent representation."

Doug's anger was rising fast. He knew all the things Howard was telling Jaclin's lawyer, but hearing everything laid out like that, in such a matter-of-fact way, with Jaclin sitting there pretending to be the innocent little victim—that, now. That was cheesing him off.

Jaclin's lawyer smiled faintly. "Yet," he said, leaning forward, "As I understand it, the changes to Mr. McNally senior's will actually benefit your client, Douglas McNally. And to the exclusion of his own brother. I wonder what a judge will make of that."

Howard smiled coldly. "That whole matter has been referred to Mr. McNally senior's own lawyer who plans to bring in neutral observers to determine whether Mr. McNally senior understood what he was signing and knew what he was agreeing to. My client Douglas McNally had no part in the attempt to get his father to change his will. The nursing home administrators are prepared to testify to that. And both Mr. Nichols and Mrs. Gardner have testified to the facts of the attempt."

"But don't you find it odd that it's your client who will benefit," Jaclin's lawyer persisted.

"I agree how odd it is. But the facts will show that Mr. McNally had no knowledge of the new will or how it was obtained. So we can only wonder why Mr. McNally is the beneficiary. In court, I am prepared to argue a clear connection between this incidence of fraudulent pretense and Mrs. McNally's reluctance to go through with the divorce proceedings my client has initiated against her."

You planned to wait til the old man croaked, Doug thought at Jaclin. Then you planned to get going on the divorce, and help yourself to a big piece of the pie.

And—the thought made him miserable—drag Gina Prine into it to muddy the waters about who in the divorce was at fault.

Howard gave the lawyer across the table a challenging stare. "Mr. McNally is also prepared to visit his father and strongly urge him to restore the will to what he originally wanted. The old will cuts my client out almost completely from any financial gain." Howard neatened the pile of papers in front of him. He waited.

"Mrs. McNally is prepared to agree to the divorce, providing your client agrees to drop charges against her," said Jaclin's lawyer.

Howard looked to Doug, who gave him a curt nod back.

"Done, but I must stipulate that Mrs. McNally must withdraw any claim to Mr. McNally's Currituck Cove property, paid for from a bequest by his mother and so excluded from marital property."

Doug knew from that other meeting with Jaclin's divorce lawyer how chancy a claim this was. He'd known right away what a mistake he'd made, buying the golf course property without the divorce. Howard had warned him. Doug had been a dunce. I'm a dunce, he told himself.

Jaclin's lawyer looked to his client.

Jaclin bit her lower lip and shot Doug a hateful glance.

Aha, thought Doug. And now here's the real Jaclin.

In spite of his sudden fear she would fight him over the golf villa, Jaclin nodded. Too afraid I'll have her thrown in jail, thought Doug. That's what she deserves. Too bad she's going to escape it.

"We'll agree to that," said her lawyer.

"As for the rest of the property, the marital property such as the house in Charlotte, my client is prepared to allow the judge to make an equitable distribution."

"We agree," said Jaclin's lawyer. With a little flounce of her head, Jaclin nodded again.

"Then I think this meeting has come to a satisfactory conclusion," said Howard, and stood. So did Doug. So did Jaclin's lawyer.

Jaclin sat with her lower lip stuck out in a pout. "But I get custody of Pompom," she snarled.

"I concede," said Doug. "Take the dog, and I'll withdraw my complaint to Animal Control that Pompom bit my grandchild."

Jaclin and her lawyer marched out of the conference room.

"About the son and grandchild," Howard began. "We need to talk about that."

Doug could finally relax. "Yes, let's talk about that. Something good for a change."

"You believe this man is your son?"

"I do," said Doug firmly.

"I'd be happier with a paternity test," said Howard.

"Not gonna ask him for one," said Doug.

It's over, he thought. The Jaclin nightmare is over.

He broke out into a big grin.

Howard just shook his head, but when he turned aside, Doug saw he was trying to suppress a grin of his own.

Then Doug's happiness died away, and the rage came back. "So let me get this straight. Jaclin gets off scot-free for essentially kidnapping my son and his family. Maybe I should file some kind of complaint about that."

"Doug," said Howard with a sigh. "It's a gray area. It will open an entire new can of worms. You're getting what you want. Maybe leave it alone."

"Okay," Doug said after a moment. "Okay. At least Jaclin is out of my life. And so is Pompom."

Fetch, Bingo!

"AM I DOING THE RIGHT thing?" Gina mourned to her two friends.

In an hour, Fran was driving Bunny to the Norfolk airport, to put her on a plane to yet another Adorable Me sales conference.

"In Paris," Fran had said to Gina, amazement in her eyes.

Fran had quit her job at the bank. In a month, she'd be married.

"A late October wedding!" said Gina with a sigh of happiness. "It can be so beautiful that time of year."

"It can get raw and ugly, though," said Fran. She shrugged. "Oh, well. It's what worked with Nelson's schedule. If the weather is bad, we have an alternate location picked out."

"If the weather cooperates, a wedding on the beach!" Now it was Bunny's turn to sigh. "Of course, that's gonna be a hair and makeup challenge, no matter how great the weather turns out. But I've got your back, Fran. You know that."

They exchanged grins. "Always," said Fran.

Now they turned to Gina, to answer her question.

"Yes, you're doing the right thing," said Fran firmly. "I know it's a jolt, selling your house, a place where you've been happy." Fran did know. She'd just sold her own. "The mountains are stunning, though, and you deserve a change."

"Much as it pains me to agree, yes, I agree," said Bunny.

It had taken a while, but gradually, the gossip about Doug Mc-Nally's marital woes, and Amelia Gardner's shoddy place in them, had leaked out, small-town gossip being what it was. It was probably no accident that Amelia and her family had pulled up stakes for a long vacation somewhere. Florida?

Doesn't matter where, thought Gina, as long as it's not here. Good riddance.

Nobody was breathing a word about Gina and Doug, though. Fran and Bunny sure weren't talking. Neither was Doug himself, or while he'd been around, Theo.

Still, Gina and Doug inhabited the same small town. They caught sight of each other from time to time. How could they help it? When they did, they turned around and headed in opposite directions.

It was a nice moment, meeting Doug's son and his family.

Then, right away, those good feelings got swept up in the confrontation with Amelia. Satisfying as it was, that's all Gina thought about, when she thought back to that moment. Not Doug's eyes, as he had looked into hers, and his apology.

Oh, in the middle of the night, she might have waked up and thought about it from time to time.

All that's history, she told herself firmly. It's over. Time for a new chapter in my life.

A few others in town might have connected all the drama surrounding Doug with Gina, like Amelia's friend Connie.

Who cares what people like that think? Gina told herself. I'm running towards something, not running away. Not like last time, when I moved to Currituck Cove to get away from that mess I was in.

As many times as she said that to herself, she couldn't quite make herself believe it.

She shrugged. She was doing it, and that was that. Her house was on the market. What she hadn't sold at the yard sale, she'd hauled off to the consignment shop or to Goodwill.

The only objects she really cared about, her art, she had carefully packed away, ready for the move.

And now she had moved into Bunny's house until her own sold.

Her realtor had come to her just the other day to tell her about two very promising nibbles.

Still—to leave the beach!

Instead of more doleful looks, she turned a smile on Bunny. "Have a blast in Paris. Geez! Paris!"

"I will," Bunny promised.

Gina looked doubtfully at the large mound of luggage piled around Bunny's feet, but she didn't say anything. Bunny could never travel anywhere without her entire beauty regimen accompanying her, and that included clothes for any and every possible occasion.

"Be a good doggie for Gina," Bunny said, bending down and fondling Bingo's ears. Bingo was a very smart dog. He knew very well what all the luggage meant. He turned sorrowful eyes on Bunny.

"Man," said Gina. "I'm going to miss you and Fran when I move," she told Bunny. "But you know who else? Bingo." She too bent over Bingo to give him hugs and kisses.

"When I get back from Paris, I may have a little surprise for you," Bunny told her, eyes twinkling.

Before Gina could cajole the secret out of Bunny, Fran was hustling Bunny out of the house. Fran and Gina got Bunny's luggage down to the curb and into Fran's car.

Gina and Bingo stood waving goodbye as Fran pulled out of Bunny's driveway.

"There they go, Bingo," said Gina. "Don't worry. She'll be back before you know it. In the meantime, you and I are gonna have fun."

Bunny would be gone for ten days. Gina and Bingo did have fun, taking long walks on the beach, splashing in the surf, Gina tossing a ball or stick for Bingo to bring back, barking excitedly for more. "Fetch, Bingo!" she'd cry, and Bingo was off like a shot.

Around a week into Bunny's Paris adventure, Gina's house sold. She went down to the realtor's office to sign all the paperwork.

It was a relief. So she told herself.

When Bunny got home, the three friends would have a good time together for one more week, then Gina would head to the mountains to go house-hunting, then she'd be back for Fran's wedding, and—that would be that.

Oh, of course she promised to come back for visits, and meant those promises. She extracted promises from Fran and Bunny to visit her, too.

This is actually, thought Gina, pretty exciting.

Two days before Bunny's return, disaster struck.

Gina and Bingo were out for their twilight walk along the beach. Gina, as always, had let Bingo off the leash for a last loping, frolicking run.

But when she called for him, he didn't come back.

He kept running.

As he dwindled down the beach, she started to run, too.

After many minutes, she had to stop, bending over with a stitch in her side, panting. No use. Bingo could easily out-run her. And he did. And he didn't come back.

She made her way back to Bunny's beach house as fast as she could. By this time she was limping, and panting not just because she was out of breath, but through genuine panic.

If anything happened to Bingo!

Do I call Animal Control? she wondered, practically hyperventilating.

By now the twilight had deepened. It was almost dark, and a dark night, too, with no moon.

Before she called anyone, she decided on one last try. Bingo was a good dog. He did know his way home. He could be heading home that very minute, through with his frolic.

Suppose he ran for the highway! Suppose something happened to him in the surf! she thought. With an effort, she suppressed her fears. Nah, labs are water dogs. They can swim like a fish. She stepped out onto Bunny's front porch.

Far up the beach she spotted a figure. Could it be Bingo? As the figure neared, she saw she was seeing two figures, person and dog. Probably not Bingo. Probably someone else out walking his dog.

The dog was straining on his leash, pulling his owner along.

As they came closer, "Oh, thank god!" Gina exclaimed. Bingo! Someone had found him, and Bingo, smart dog, was showing him how to get Bingo home.

Closer still.

Gina flung herself off the porch.

Bingo and Doug.

"Bingo!" she cried.

"Bingo found me," Doug told her. "I was walking way up the beach, this shape in the twilight runs past me, whirls around, comes at me, whines. I pick up the leash and he starts leading me where he wants me to take him."

Bingo sat in the sand, thumping his tail.

"'Course, I saw it was Bingo. I knew where he wanted me to go."

Gina kept opening her mouth to say something. Not saying it. Closing it again.

"Funny thing. It was where I wanted to go, too. I was just too chicken to do it."

"Too...chicken?" Gina faltered.

"Not sure you'd want to hear my news. Wanted desperately to tell you."

"What news?" said Gina.

"My divorce just came through," he said simply.

When she could think of nothing to say back, he stepped toward her and pulled her into his arms. He cupped her face in his hands, and lowered his face to hers.

He kissed her, slowly, sweetly, thoroughly, taking his time.

She found herself kissing him back as breathlessly as he now started kissing her.

"This time I'm, uh, prepared, too. Just in case. Just in case you'd want me, messed up as I am."

"You're messed up, Doug McNally," she agreed. "And so am I."

Love, as it turned out, was a very messy thing all around.

"Let's avoid the couch this time," she murmured, drawing him into Bunny's house, closing the door behind them. And shutting Bingo safely inside, of course.

With Bingo lying at the bottom of the stairs playing guard dog, Gina retreated step by step up the stairs.

With each step she took, Doug undid a button of her blouse.

By the time they'd gotten to the top, he had undone them all.

They swayed together at the top of the stairs as he freed her breasts from the confinement of her bra, and kissed them, the right, then the left. She grabbed the shirttail of his golf shirt and eased it over his head, marveling in the dim light at the smooth muscles of his torso and how much she wanted to press her lips against every inch of it.

He backed her toward the bedroom, toward the bed.

She fell back on it, but sat up again to undo his fly and help him pull down his jeans. Now she could act on her desire. She planted little rows of kisses down his torso, down the line of black hair from his navel into the wild curls around his erect member. To take him into her mouth while he twined his hands in her hair.

Gently, he pulled himself away from her. He turned aside and fumbled for the condom. Smoothed it on. Then he stretched out on the bed beside her. He kissed her some more on the mouth, exploring deep with his tongue, while his long slender hands probed to find the moist eager place between her legs, and penetrate with a finger.

At her cry, he slid on stop of her, pulling her hips to fit against his.

She helped him guide himself inside her, giving a gasp as he filled her, settling around him and pulling him in closer by twining her legs about his waist.

"Gina," he breathed. He gazed into her eyes, his gray eyes probing hers. "I have wanted this so long."

His thrusts were faster, more rhythmic. She felt she would lose herself; her back arched.

"Not yet," he whispered. "Let me savor you, Gina. Just a little longer."

"Now," she demanded, when she couldn't take another minute of the agonizing pleasure of it, hovering on the very lip of pleasure, and he thrust deep. She went over with a cry.

He followed, hard, then released with his own cry in a long series of shuddering thrusts.

They lay limply together. He stroked her and murmured into her ear, she wasn't sure what.

He murmured her name, "Gina. Gina."

She lay across his broad chest, pillowing her face against him, her eyes slits of contentment.

They both dozed.

She woke with a start. He was propped up on an elbow, a finger tenderly tracing her cheek down the line of her jaw.

"Wish I were a painter," he said. "I'd paint you just like this."

She smiled into his eyes.

"Gina," he said, flipping over on his stomach and stroking her with his hands.

"What's that, Doug."

"I don't want you to leave."

"Don't let's spoil this moment by talking about that."

"Okay. Tomorrow?"

"Promise," she said.

In the morning, the sun woke them. She hopped out of bed.

He woke too, reaching for her with a groan. "Don't go. Come back to bed."

"Bingo," she said, grabbing for her clothes.

After Bingo's brisk morning walk, she came back to Bunny's front porch, dumping the sand out of her shoes and brushing Bingo off.

Inside, the house was silent. She tiptoed upstairs, and stood looking down at Doug's inert form. Asleep, she told herself.

His hand snaked out and grabbed her. "Not so fast, Ms. Prine!" So then they had to have morning sex, didn't they? Fast, fun, full of laughter.

"Whew, Doug. I'm getting on in years. I may not have the stamina for this," she said, teasing him, running a nail down his torso.

"Breakfast?" he said hopefully. "Just not that thing. Ugh. With the egg in the juice."

She giggled. "All I have is cereal."

"Cereal's good."

"And o.j. without the egg."

"And coffee?"

"And coffee," she promised. "It's already brewing."

Later they sat together in Bunny's breakfast nook. He kept reaching for her, touching her.

"I'm scared if I take my hands off you, you'll disappear."

"You know I have to leave," she said, looking over at him ruefully. "I said yes to that job. I'm due to start in two weeks. Bunny comes back tomorrow, I hang around for a week, then I'm out of here."

"Spend that last week at my house," he urged. "Theo's gone. My friend Alberto just left. It will be the two of us and no one else."

"Okay," she said, and dimpled up.

"While you're there, maybe I can convince you."

"Convince me of what?"

"Marry me, Gina."

"Doug." She turned aside, troubled.

"I know, I know. What's the phrase? The ink's not even dry on my divorce? But I've been thinking about this for a long time."

"We only met last spring."

"And now it's fall. I guess if we were younger, maybe everyone would tell us to take it slow. But we're not, are we? I want to spend the good years with you, Gina."

"I don't know what to say. I've sold my house. I'm moving to the mountains."

"We can figure something out. We don't have children. Well, I do, as it turns out. But no one we'd inconvenience, no lives we'd uproot. Just our own."

"What would you do, Doug? You've told me your golf career is over."

"I've been thinking about that. My situation is solid, thanks to Theo and a good lawyer. And, you know, over the last few months, I haven't just sat around on my ass. I've been setting up something interesting, Gina."

"What's that."

"I, uh, didn't make the greatest impression with the golf club when I first got here. As you may recall."

Gina had to work not to let her mouth quirk up into a smile. "I remember."

"So I have redeemed myself with the board. I realized there's no place in this whole county for young kids to learn about golf. So I set up a golf camp. Can't try it out until next year, but the club board has approved my plans. And I'll run it. The club board thinks it will attract visitors to the resort, too. While the adults are out playing golf and having fun, their kids will be learning the game."

"That's a great idea!"

"I know. Everyone loves me now. Except. Um. Maybe Mrs. Soo. My next door neighbor," he reminded her. "I don't think she has forgiven me yet. Oh," he said, snapping his fingers. "How could I forget. I got you something, when I was in England that time."

"The time you met your son."

"Yeah. Wait right here." He whisked into Bunny's living room and came back with a little package. "Here. I brought this along just in case I ginned up the courage to find you at Bunny's house."

While Doug poured himself another cup of coffee, and one for her, Gina unwrapped his package.

Lying spread out on the plain wrapping paper, she saw some pieces of crystal. One was a deep amber. Another, a rich brown.

"What are these?"

"These," he said, leaning over them and fingering them, "come from an ore called Cassiterite. Tin, Gina. This is what crystals from tin ore look like. They're kinda fragile, but the people I talked to in Cornwall and Devon say they've heard these crystals make great gemstones."

"Unique," Gina murmured.

"I learned about them by studying the ancient Romans. Did you know they called the British Isles the Cassiterides? The Tin Isles?"

"I didn't know you were interested in history," said Gina.

"I am. Very. And I thought about your Celtic designs, and I thought, what if Gina made jewelry out of all sorts of gems and minerals from different places and different historical periods? Then I saw these."

"Wow, Doug. All that time, you were thinking about me, and what I'm interested in, and looking for something I'd like that would fit that."

"I was."

"As for me, I still don't know much about golf. Just what Theo taught me when we watched those tournaments."

"But I'm not just interested in golf. I'll bet there are things we're both interested in."

"Like these." Gina stirred the crystals with a fingertip.

He smiled. "Gina. Let's agree to try, between us. We have something great. Let's not lose it."

When he left, she had promised to think about it.

"What do you think, Bingo?" Gina asked, looking after Doug as he jogged up the beach.

Bingo thumped his tail hard against the planks of the porch.

"I'd call that the Bingo Seal of Approval," said Gina. "Now tell me something. How did you know to find Doug and bring him to me?"

Bingo wasn't saying.

Slo-mo

"THIS AIN'T RIGHT, BUD," said Theo, as Doug drove him out of Norfolk and turned onto the highway that would take them to Currituck Cove.

"Get outta here," said Doug. "Of course it's right."

"From what you're telling me, the second the ink was dry on your divorce—"

Doug winced at the expression.

"—you and Gina fell into each other's arms."

Doug smiled at the images that conjured up. Gina in his arms. Kissing Gina. Burying himself in the sweetness that was Gina—"

"Geez, man, want me to drive?"

"Sorry, Theo. I'll pay attention. Promise."

"Please do, or we won't live long enough for you to get me back to your place and me to make an ass of myself."

"Theo. You aren't making an ass of yourself."

"Why didn't you tell me? Why didn't you say no to me?"

"Because I always want you visiting me. You know. It's a mi casa, su casa kind of a thing. You know the drill."

"Doug." Theo's voice was patient. "I'll be a third wheel. I'll be a killjoy. You've got Gina in your house. You two need your privacy to, you know, cavort around and whatnot."

"It's a big place, Theo. I put you in the far bedroom. It'll be fine. You're like my brother, Theo," Doug turned around to say. "The brother I wish I had."

"Doug!"

"Sorry."

"Eyes on the road, dammit."

"Sorry."

When they got to his house in the golf community, there was Gina to throw open the front door and come running down the flagstone path to cast herself into Theo's arms. "Theo!"

"Hey, Gina!"

He noticed a severe woman in a sun-hat, hovering on the porch of the golf villa next door, her mouth pressed into a thin line, her eyes disapproving.

"Oh, her. That's the president of the Doug Fan Club."

"Oh lord," said Theo, remembering.

Doug gave a sheepish shrug. "Hi, Mrs. Soo," he called over the woman.

She didn't answer, just disappeared inside her own house.

"Some people, you get off on the wrong foot with them, you never get it back," said Doug.

Theo and Gina rolled their eyes.

"I saw that," said Doug. "Let's get you inside, Theo. Let's get a drink into that hand."

After a dinner Doug and Gina whipped up together, they all sat on the patio as the dusk came on.

"I'm happy for you two," said Theo. But he noticed Gina looking uncomfortable.

"It has been a happy time," said Gina only.

"Gina won't give me a definite yes to my very persistent question," said Doug. "But Gina's a big girl. She can make up her own mind. I'm just trying to pamper her into a state of insensibility so she'll say it against her better judgment."

"Next week I leave for the mountains," she told Theo. "I've already postponed my start date at the gallery a week longer than I should. I've got to get myself up there."

"Doug told me," said Theo. "You're going to be great at managing a gallery. Time for your own art, too, I hope?"

"Plenty of time for that. It's the best part of the job. Speaking of that. We're still on with Len, tomorrow?" she leaned over to Doug to say.

"Yep. We're going to see another one of those artists, tomorrow, Theo. Remember our art field trips?"

"How could I forget?" said Theo.

"Well, once Gina helped me hang and place all the art," said Doug, waving his hand around. "We saw there was one empty wall that just begged for a big painting, and Gina says she knows the very guy. We're heading out to see his stuff tomorrow."

Theo gazed around, admiring the pieces in the dining room. "I remember these so well, where we were when we picked out each one. After dinner, take me on a tour so I can see all the rest?"

After dinner, they did.

The next day, breakfast over, they piled into Doug's car to head out into the country to the studio of a man named Len West, a man Gina said was the best around. "I remember we tried to see him when we were going on those field trips," she told the other two. "But he was doing a residency at some art colony out of state."

They pulled up to a low-slung farmhouse in the middle of a meadow of late fall wildflowers. They piled out of the car.

A man stood in the doorway of the house, waving them in. "This way," he called. "Len West," he said, shaking Doug's hand. He was lean and rugged-looking. He looked more like a farmer than an artist. He had a soft Southern accent and piercing eyes, hazel, Gina thought, looking into his interesting face, all planes and jutting nose.

He and Doug headed to the back of the farmhouse and Len's studio. Gina trailed behind, and then, behind her, slowly, Theo.

Gina and Theo stood silent, watching, while Len showed Doug several of his pieces, huge canvases that would take up that whole empty wall. Amazing canvases blazing with shape and color, thick with texture.

Doug strolled back to his friends, Len at his side, speaking rapidly to him.

"Astonishing, isn't it?" he said to Gina. He turned to Len. "When the three of us first started looking at art, I didn't know what I liked. I'd never thought about it. These two knew what they were looking at. Gina's an artist herself, and Theo—that's my friend Theo—has always had a good eye. But now I know what I like, and I like your stuff. Very, very much."

"Thank you," said Len in his soft-at-the-edges voice. "Gina I know." He gave her a lop-sided grin, and she smiled back. "And Theo—your friend?"

"Theo's the brother I never had," said Doug, beaming. "What do you think? I think I might love that big one with the reds best, but it's hard to pick just one."

Theo was standing silent, staring. Not saying anything at all.

Doug found himself talking prices with Len almost right away. When Len mentioned a figure, Doug whipped out his checkbook on the spot.

"You've been quiet, Theo," he said, coming back to Theo and Gina. He dropped his voice. "Think I made the wrong choice?"

"Huh?" Theo jolted with a start out of whatever place he'd gone to. "Uh. No. Your paintings are brilliant," he said past them to Len.

What's going on, thought Doug. Something's wrong. Theo doesn't sound right.

But he needed to talk to Len about when and how he could get the painting to Doug's golf villa. It was too big for the car. He figured he'd find out later what was going on with Theo.

"Okay, that about covers it," he told Len. "I love your stuff. Thanks again. Okay, you two." He turned to Theo and Gina. "We passed a great little lunch place back down the road. Let's head in that direction."

As they left Len's farmhouse, left Len standing in the door of it, Doug realized Theo was lagging behind. Theo had turned completely around. He had locked eyes with Len West.

"Okay," said Doug in an undertone to Gina. "Something is going on with Theo. I wonder if he's sick?"

Gina glanced behind them at where Theo stood transfixed in the middle of the wildflowers. She turned back to Doug. "You know how Theo is always telling you that you're thick? Well, he's right, Doug. Thick." She poked him in the ribs. "Don't stare."

Doug made his way to the car, and he and Gina got in. "Really?"

"Really," she said, grinning.

In a moment, Theo followed them. Silently, he let himself into the back seat.

"Seatbelt, Theo?" said Gina.

"Oh. Oh, yes. Right," said Theo in a stifled voice Doug didn't think he'd ever heard before.

"Bro. Why don't you stay here and browse through Len's art. Maybe you'll find something you'd like for yourself. We'll pick you up after lunch, and we promise to bring back takeout for you."

Without a word, Theo bolted out of the car, heading back to Len, and Len was holding his door wide.

"You know those shampoo commercials, where one person is kind of bounding through a field of wildflowers in slo-mo toward another?" said Gina dreamily. "I think we just saw that scene playing out in real life, right before our eyes." Then she poked Doug and guffawed. "Maybe you'll find something you'd like for yourself," she mimicked.

Doug laughed til he cried. He could barely drive them to the lunch place, he was laughing so hard. "My, my. Theo, the man with a heart of stone."

Gina gave him a look he couldn't decipher.

But Doug hoped what they had noticed was right. He hoped Theo saw what he liked, and acted on it. He was happy. He wanted Theo to be happy too. He wanted the whole world to be happy, but especially Theo.

It seemed so. Doug and Gina didn't see much of Theo that week. Theo's worry that he would invade their privacy turned out to be bootless. Theo didn't have time to invade anyone's privacy, even if he had wanted to.

Doug insisted that Theo borrow his car, and every day, Theo headed down the highway to bliss.

By the end of the week, Theo had changed his entire life plan. He was going to stay in Currituck Cove. He already knew he could do his job from anywhere in the world. Why not here, with the man he loved? He and Len became a couple.

"You accuse me of making a snap decision," Doug grumbled to Gina. "What about those two."

The two of them couldn't pry him away from Len. But Doug did have some business he needed to conduct, loose ends from the last stormy months he wanted to run by Theo, so of course Theo made time for that.

Gina tactfully found something else to do, and Doug and Theo sat out on the patio with beers, talking it over.

"So," Doug concluded. "Everything ended well. Trey Nichols is headed for jail. Jaclin isn't, because I declined to press charges, so she had to give me everything I asked for."

"She still got half the Charlotte house. Didn't deserve it."

"Maybe not. But I don't want to descend to her level. I don't want to take anyone to the cleaners, as the expression goes. The judge decided on an equitable distribution, and I signed off on it. Meanwhile, Jaclin didn't fight me on the golf villa."

"Well, I agree. Everything worked out well," said Theo. "What about your dad?"

"That's a little less satisfying. I really don't know how all that shook out. The court appointed a neutral panel to look into dad's will and what he really might have wanted to do with it. Howard asked me what I would consider the best outcome. I said let the old codger put it back the way it was. Give his money to some organization."

"That's a lot of money, bro."

"Yeah. The place he wants it to go to, I guess he must have some good memories, must have spent some good times there with friends. Any friends he did have there, anyone he used to know there, my guess is they're dead or just as dotty as he is. But that's what he wanted."

"Oh, you know what he really wanted."

"To stick it to me and Stan. God knows why. Look, Theo, it's not as if I'd turn up my nose at the money. It would be nice to have that kind of money. When is it not? But I don't have to have it to be happy. I know what I have to have, to be happy, and money ain't it. Time will tell whether I ever get it."

"She loves you, man."

"I think she does. Is that enough, though? I guess I'll find out. Anyhow, what steams me is that Stan is the one who could really use Dad's money. There's no justice. He wouldn't have even gotten it with the fraudulent will."

"Stan's an addict, Doug. If he got that kind of money, it would all go up his nose. You know that. Up his nose unless and until it kills him first."

"I guess. I do know that if Dad owes it to anyone, he owes it to Stan. So. I don't know if Dad ended up changing his will back, and I won't know until he finally does drop dead. I'm figuring at that point the money will all go to the Northern Virginia Snooty Gentleman's Society, or whatever the hell it's called. The dementia's getting worse, though. Dad was in the general population at the nursing home. I got a letter saying they wanted to move him to the memory unit, and I approved it. Someone, his lawyer I guess, did persuade him to give me power of attorney, so I've had to spend a lot of time straightening out his rat's nest of bills and expenses."

Theo made time for his friends again a few afternoons later, because he was as curious as Doug was. Bunny, Gina's friend, had some surprise she was about to spring on Gina. Their other friend, Fran, seemed to be in on it too.

"Guess it's some kind of going-away present for Gina," said Doug.

"She's really leaving?" said Theo.

"Looks like it." Doug felt morose, especially as the day to say goodbye drew near.

"But you two are perfect for each other. You're so happy together. I've never seen you so happy, Doug."

"Likewise, my man. We're two happy dudes."

Theo beamed.

"But," said Doug, "Gina is a determined lady, and going to the mountains is what she's determined to do."

"You two ready?" said Gina, popping into the room.

"Sure," said Doug. "Where's this place Bunny wants us to meet her?"

"I have directions on my phone," said Gina.

They headed out down the coast. At a small road, barely a road at all, more like a weedy path, they turned inland and bumped along it in Doug's car.

"You sure this is the right way?" said Doug.

"I guess so," said Gina. "That's what the phone—oh, look. There's the hotpinkmobile, over there. That's gotta be the place."

They turned into a fenced yard and got out.

Bunny and Fran were there to welcome them, grinning.

"What's going on?" said Gina. "Think you'll finally tell me?"

"Love is in the air, Gina," said Bunny, mysteriously.

"I'll say it is," said Doug.

"You and Doug," said Fran, smiling mischievously. Doug hadn't thought Fran liked him much, but slowly, that seemed to have changed. Bunny, though. She'd always liked him.

"Yeah, you and Doug," said Bunny to Gina. "And now, looks like, Theo has found himself an amazing guy."

Theo blushed.

"But you and Theo aren't the only guys in love."

As Bunny said this, a tall, spare woman stepped out to the front porch of the small house they'd come to, down the end of a gravel drive.

"Hi, y'all," she said to them all. "Come on in the house and meet the proud mama."

Doug and Gina looked at each other, puzzled.

From the inside of the house came an excited yipping.

Theo began to laugh. "And who, may I ask, Miss Bunny, is the proud papa?"

"Why, Bingo, of course!" said Bunny.

The woman threw the door wide, and they all looked in. Beyond a mesh baby gate stood a very lovely Labrador Retriever bitch and her brood of squirming pups. Six, by Doug's count.

"Four yellow lab pups and two black ones. If you want chocolate, 'fraid you're outta luck. Got none of those, this litter."

Doug found himself inching closer to the baby gate and peering over. Beside him, he could feel Gina trembling.

"Those are Bingo's pups," Bunny told her. "And Fran and I decided the best going-away present ever, Ms. Gina Prine, would be one of Bingo's pups."

Gina burst into tears.

Doug was busy soothing her, which was a good thing, because he was feeling the prick of tears behind his own eyelids. So unmanly.

Theo was shaking his head at him.

"What do you think, Gina," he murmured. "A yellow lab? A black lab?"

"A black lab!" she cried.

"So, ma'am, here we got the little lady black lab, and there's the little fellow. Take your pick."

"Can I have them all?" Gina quavered.

Bunny hugged her. "Girl or boy?"

"They're both adorable. But I want one exactly like Bingo, and since there never will be a dog exactly like Bingo, the closest one."

When they left, little Bongo was hers. But Bongo wasn't ready to leave his mama.

"As soon as I get back here for your wedding, Fran, I'll come get him."

Bright eyes

FRAN'S WEDDING WENT off beautifully. "Perfectly," Bunny pronounced, wiping mascara off her cheeks.

On a completely calm, magnificent late October day, Nelson and Fran stood on the beach together, while a beaming Father Laughton read them their rites (Bunny's words).

Bunny and Gina, in frilly dresses, along with Nelson's daughter Deanie May, were the bridesmaids.

Theo, still in Currituck Cove, was there to witness the happy event, and so was Len West. Doug was there.

Gina had never been in such a great wedding. In her experience, something always went wrong, and you just had to roll with it.

"But yours, Fran!" she gushed, afterward. "Perfection!"

Doug had suggested they hold their reception in the golf club's Great Room. In the end, though, Nelson and Fran had gone for the tacky splendor of the Dolphin Room at the Seaforest.

"God, Gina," Doug leaned over to her to say. "This place. It gives me goosebumps."

"Doesn't it, though? It's where we met."

"I've missed you, these last weeks. Liking it up there?"

"Yeah, the mountains are beautiful. I don't know which I love more, mountains or beach." It tugged at her heart, though, to be back at the beach. And to be with Doug. She had missed him even more than she'd expected to.

She and Doug were sitting together at one of the Dolphin Room's little round tables. Doug stood up and waved. "There they are," he said.

Theo and Len came over, and Gina made them sit down at their table.

"How's the plan?" she asked Theo with a grin.

"It's coming along great," said Theo. He and Len exchanged a long soulful look.

"Get a room, guys," Doug joshed them.

Len blushed. Theo laughed. "You've gotta know how to take this guy," he explained to Len. "There's just one problem," he said after a moment. "I'm looking to buy something in Currituck Cove. Not out near Len's place. The wifi isn't good enough out there, and for my business, I need good wifi. Our idea, I'll buy us a place in town, and then Len will use his whole house as studio space."

"I've needed to expand for a while," said Len softly.

"Great idea," said Gina.

"There's a hitch, though," said Theo.

"A hitch?" she asked.

"I've found the perfect place. Dunno if the owner will sell, though."

"Make him an offer he can't refuse. Horse head in his bed, all that," said Doug.

"I've thought about that. I don't think that will move him. I'm guessing something else might."

"Good luck with it, Theo," said Gina.

After a while, Theo and Len rose to leave. Theo leaned over and gave Gina a kiss. "What about it?" he whispered in her ear. "What are you going to do about Doug?"

Doug had just excused himself to go to the men's room.

"I remember you asking me that same thing one time before, Theo," she said. "And in those same words."

"I remember that, too. Doug is eating his heart out over you, Gina. You've spoiled him for anyone else, you know that, don't you?"

"I've taken on some serious obligations, Theo," said Gina. "And I'm serious about my art."

"I know you are," said Theo. "I hear that. I have serious obligations, too. But, you know. A balance can be reached. It's not impossible. You just have to want it."

He kissed her on the cheek. Then he and Len made their way over to Fran to offer their congratulations, and left the party.

I need some air, thought Gina. She stood too, and drifted to the little balcony off the Dolphin Room, looking out over the sea.

A brilliant moon cast a bright streak of silver across the waves. Across the sky, it was as if a giant hand had thrown a magnificent sweep of stars.

She felt someone beside her. She knew without turning around. It was Doug. She realized how well she knew him now. The feel of him, the scent of him even.

"Gina," he said at her ear. "Theo has just made me the most remarkable offer."

"Oh?" she turned to him and he placed both hands lightly on her shoulders.

"Theo wants to buy my beach place. If I sell to him, I thought I'd buy somewhere else. But my decision really is someone else's decision."

"Whose, Doug?" she could barely get out the words.

"Yours, Gina. Will you marry me? If you tell me yes, I'll move to the mountains. The golf program for kids is on a solid footing here. I have a good idea whom I'd recommend the club hire to replace me. I've done good work for the club, getting the program going. You know, there's golf in the mountains, too. I can find something up there. And, you're up there."

She was silent.

"Anyway, Gina. Tomorrow you're due to pick up Bongo, and, well, can I live without you? Maybe I can. I may not be able to live without Bongo."

She punched him in the ribs. He put his arms around her and drew her close to him. "I ache for you, Gina."

What do I say? she thought. What do I want? She brought his hands to her lips and kissed them.

"What's your answer, Gina Prine?" He swiveled her around and pulled her hard against him.

Leaning back against his chest, encircled by his arms, she looked out over the balcony, wondering at the sea. The stars. "I was thinking, today, when Nelson and Fran promised to love each other til death do they part, what a beautiful thought that is. But there's another beautiful old phrase from the marriage ceremony. Nobody uses it any more. 'With my body I thee worship.' I've always thought that sounded sorta pagan. But until the last couple of months, I never realized it was in there because—" Her hands tightened on his, and she took a deep, shuddering breath. "Because it's just true."

Doug fished around in his pocket and drew out a little box. Flipped it open. The glint of moonlight turned the diamond on the ring inside to white fire. "A jewel for the jeweler," he murmured in her ear, as she gazed down at the little box and its contents.

"Turn around, Gina. Turn around and give me your answer."

"My answer?" The answer that had always been there, waiting under the layers of self-doubt and mistrust, rose up inside her. The joy burst out of her. "Yes!"

Their bright eyes were filled with the moon, with the stars, the surge of the ocean as the waves came rolling in. Their eyes were filled with each other.

When they left the balcony to go in, they went straight through the hotel lobby toward the parking lot, too dazzled, too many stars in their eyes to notice the big garish sign perched on the registration desk.

TOMORROW NITE!
KARAOKE NITE!
FALL IN LOVE. WE DARE YOU.
IT'S THE BEACH!

Don't miss out!

Use the link below to sign up for Lucinda's newsletter. And get Book 2 of the **Love's a Beach** series:
BIG PACKAGE FOR BUNNY
An age-difference romance with steam, small-town beach vibes, and a mouthy parrot—including a side order of STEM!
Then move on to Book 3:
Storm Flags Flying, Deanie May
An enemies-to-lovers, fake engagement romance with more of that small-town beach steam, plus the sneakiest of sneaky cats!
https://lucindawritesromance.com/contact/

ABOUT LUCINDA

HI, EVERYONE. I WRITE romance under the pen name Lucinda McFall. So who is Lucinda, actually? "Lucinda" is the first name of one of my great-grandmothers. "McFall" is the last name of another one of my great-grandmothers. I am Lucinda!

But my real name is Jane Wiseman. I split my time between very urban Minneapolis and the Sandia Mountains of New Mexico. Minneapolis is a vibrant city, and I love living there. The Sandias, though—they are ROMANCE. That's Lucinda's true home.

To find out more about Lucinda's books, including an ebook version of this novel, go to:

https://lucindawritesromance.com

FIND JANE'S BOOKS (fantasy, science fiction, dystopia), at https://janemwiseman.com

Don't miss out!

Visit the website below and you can sign up to receive emails whenever Lucinda McFall publishes a new book. There's no charge and no obligation.

https://books2read.com/r/B-A-SZVT-BIWYB

BOOKS 2 READ

Connecting independent readers to independent writers.

Also by Lucinda McFall

Love's a Beach
Karaoke Nite at the Love Club
Big Package for Bunny
Storm Flags Flying, Deanie May

Tangled Web
That Fraudster Love